VAMPIRE GIRL

D1407763

VAMPIRE GIRL

Karpov Kinrade

DARING BOOKS

KarpovKinrade.com
Copyright © 2016 Karpov Kinrade
Cover Art Copyright © 2016 Karpov Kinrade

~~~~~

Published by Daring Books

~~~~~

Hardback Edition

~~~~~

ISBN-10: 193955943X
ISBN-13: 9781939559432

~~~~~

First Edition

~~~~~

ISBN-10: 1939559421
ISBN-13: 9781939559425

License Notes

You may not use, reproduce or transmit in any manner, any part of this book without written permission, except in the case of brief quotations used in critical articles and reviews, or in accordance with federal Fair Use laws. All rights are reserved.

Disclaimer

This is a work of fiction. Names, characters, places and incidents are products of the author's imagination, or the author has used them fictitiously.

For anyone who dreams of taking the Blood Oath.
The Princes of Hell are coming for you.
Are you ready?

TABLE OF CONTENTS

1

THE ROXY

"We are the oasis in the desert, the safe harbor in the storm, the place anyone is welcome, as long as you're not a jerk to the servers."
—Arianna Spero

The rain falls in sheets, like layered waterfalls outside my second story window. I hug my knees to my chest and press my cheek against the cool glass as I watch the world outside soak itself in the Oregon mist and water.

My mom is downstairs cooking something that smells wonderful. Waffles and bacon, I think. My favorites. Breakfast for lunch? Or would it be dinner? Working graveyard messes my whole schedule up. I check the clock. It's nearly three in the afternoon, so maybe linner? Or dunch? I chuckle at my own stupid humor. I've been an adult now for fifteen hours. I was born at midnight on a full moon during a storm, or so my mom tells me.

There are day people and night people. I am a night person. An owl. A vampire. A being of darkness. A moon goddess.

I hear my mom shuffling around the kitchen, humming the nameless tune she always hums when she's alone. I feel a strange kind of melancholy today, but I don't know why. It's my birthday. I should be happy. Why aren't I?

I tug on the oversized shirt I sleep in, pulling it down my shins as I shiver. The heater is on the fritz again, just in time for a very cold winter.

"Ari! Breakfast!" My mom's voice is shrill. Forced frivolity. She's been on edge too, likely from those final notice bills I saw in her room.

She doesn't know I've dropped out of college to work full time at The Roxy. She doesn't know I already paid the electric bill in person so it wouldn't get shut off. She'll be pissed when she finds out, but at least we'll still have electricity.

College can wait.

It's not as if I'm behind, having graduated a year early and completed three semesters of undergrad classes already. But I have a long, expensive road ahead of me if I want to fulfill my dream of becoming a lawyer. And I don't have the time or money for that dream just yet. She'll understand one day.

I hope.

"Coming, Mom!"

I flip my legs off my window bench and grab a pair of jeans lying on my floor. It only takes a few seconds to pull them on and tie my long hair into a ponytail. A few black wayward strands fall out and I tuck them behind my ears and run downstairs.

My mom smiles when she sees me, but her eyes are creased with worry. "Happy Birthday, Arianna!" She's holding a plate of waffles and bacon, with eighteen lit candles sticking out of the waffles.

"Thanks, Mom." I walk over and blow out the candles, missing the last one as I run out of air. I didn't make a wish, so it doesn't really matter.

"What did you wish for?" she asks.

I smile, hoping my eyes don't betray my strange anxiety. "If I tell you, it won't come true."

She nods. "Of course." My mom and I don't look much alike. She's wild, with red curly hair, freckles, and hazel eyes. I take after my father, she says. The few pictures I've seen of him prove her right. The pale skin, black hair, elfin features, and green eyes are nearly identical. I may have gotten my looks from my father, but I get my determination and stubbornness from my mother.

She limps around the kitchen serving up our breakfast, and I resist the urge to help her, to insist she sits. I know she's in pain. I can see it eating away at her, in the pinched expressions on her face and weariness of her eyes. It's gotten worse over the years, and her pain pills are less and less effective. But despite it all, she won't let me help. My mother is nothing if not proud and fiercely independent.

We sit at our two-person plastic kitchen table surrounded by peeling yellow walls with cheap flea market paintings of flowers and fruit decorating them. I love our kitchen, as tiny and old as it is. It's cheery and always smells of cinnamon and honey.

I'm mid-bite when my mom looks up, her grin faltering. "What time do you have class today?"

I hate lying to her, but today isn't the day to tell her the truth. "It's Friday," I say. "No classes. Just work."

Her eyes light up. "Oh, maybe you could take the day off? We could go hiking? Or maybe to the museum?"

I want to say yes. I really, really do. But I can't afford to lose a day's worth of pay. Not when I know rent is overdue and we're getting eviction notices. But I can't tell her that. She works so hard to provide for us, and I know it would break her heart if she thought I was worried. So instead I shrug and try to act casual. "I can't, I'm sorry. I wouldn't be able to get anyone to cover for me this late. But how about we go out to eat after my shift? My treat."

I can see the disappointment on her face, but she covers it quickly with a smile. "That would be fun. But

I'm paying. No arguments. You only turn eighteen once."

"Deal." I take my plate to the sink and wash it, then kiss her on the cheek as I head upstairs. "I've got to get ready for work. I'll see you in the morning."

"I don't like you working these late shifts, Ari," she says as I'm halfway up the stairs. "Such strange people coming and going. It's not safe."

I stop and look at her over my shoulder. "Shari looks after us. Don't worry. I'm fine." But her words send a shudder down my spine.

If I'd known how the day would progress, I would have stayed. I would have spent every minute with her I could. I would have tried to find a way to change fate. But that's foolish thinking from a foolish girl who didn't know anything, isn't it?

...

I dress quickly in my standard black skinny jeans and tight black shirt. I wear my uncomfortable push up bra to give my breasts more cleavage than they naturally have. Better tips that way.

The only jewelry I wear is the blue sandstone ring my mother gave me when I turned thirteen. She said it's a star stone, often called 'sparkle fairy' during the Renaissance and believed to be blessed by fairies. I always wear it, and though I don't believe in the magical properties some attribute to stones, I still feel happier and luckier with it on.

I turn my attention back to my hair, pulling it into a braid, and then apply red lipstick, charcoal eye shadow and black mascara to my eyes, until I look the part of a Roxy waitress.

It's a long walk to work, and even still I'm lucky to live so close to downtown. My mom got our apartment for a steal when I was a baby—some kind of friend of a friend connection—and we've only had a few rent increases in all this time. It's the only way we can still afford to live in this part of Portland.

I know the drill as I walk, even in this friendly city. I walk with a determined gait, eyes focused, senses alerted to everything around me. Women walking alone will always be cause for caution in our world, sadly. But I'm not an inherently paranoid person, and yet my senses are on high alert.

Someone is following me.

I can't see them, or even really hear them, but someone is watching me, stalking me, and my every instinct is screaming danger.

I walk faster, my heart hammering in my chest, my palms getting sweaty. I pull pepper spray out of my bag and clutch it in my hand. I won't go quietly, whatever they think. My black boot heals click against the wet pavement. I try to quiet my breathing so I can hear if someone else approaches, but all I hear is the steady drone of rain washing the city away.

By the time I enter the crazy world-unto-its-own that is The Roxy, my thin jacket is soaked and I'm shaking, though not just from the cold. The diner is buzzing with people, and the warmth and fragrant smells set my nerves at ease like nothing else can. I peek outside, but see nothing unusual. Maybe it all was just in my head.

One of our regulars says hi, and I smile and wave, grabbing a napkin to dry my face after the rain. I enjoy the eclectic personalities that come in at all hours. I love interacting with them, finding out about their lives, giving them just what they need to get through the next few hours. I've often wished that working here was my destiny. It's not a glamorous destiny, as things go. I'd never make millions or change the world serving coffees and diner food to the caffeine-craving, sleep-deprived, hungover masses, but it's fulfilling work I enjoy. Doesn't that count for a lot? When most people dread waking up in the morning and facing their day, I think loving what you do and who you do it with is a gift. But I have never felt content in my own skin, or my own life. I always thought it was because I needed to accomplish something bigger than myself. Help others. Make a difference. I chose law thinking that would be my fit. My ticket to peace and happiness, but I'm starting to doubt there is anything in this world that can make me feel those things.

Esmeralda is in true form when I arrive, her long lashes blinking frantically. "Darlin', you are late!" she says in her southern accent I know for a fact is fake. She was born and raised in Los Angeles before moving to Oregon, but I'd never tell anyone that. She's very protective of her fictional southern roots. She tsks me, waving a long, red nail in my face. "We are nearly bursting!"

I look around and see she's right. The late shift is always crazy. Professional alcoholics know to eat before they drink, and come in to fill up. Stragglers line the counters ready for something greasy, fried, or baked to satiate whatever craving they are having, and as the night wears on, the seats will overflow. We are the oasis in the desert, the safe harbor in the storm, the place anyone is welcome, as long as you're not a jerk to the servers. Shari, the owner, makes one thing very clear: The customer is not always right, and if you disrespect her staff, you're out of here. End of story. I love her for that. I worked at a different diner before getting this job, and quit after one week. The manager treated us like indentured servants. I'm nobody's servant.

"Is Shari crazy mad?" I ask Es.

Es just rolls her eyes. "Puh-lease." She takes the napkin from my hand and dabs under my eyes. "Look up," she says, as she fixes my makeup. "Darlin', you need to get a car or learn to appreciate public transportation. This is not the weather for walking in."

Before I can argue with her, she saunters off. I sigh and look up at Jesus hanging on the cross. He always looks so reproachful, as if to say, 'You think you have problems?' but then again, maybe he's just checking out the naked sculptures behind the bar. The decor of The Roxy is nearly as famous as the cheeky staff and artery scorching foods. I run to the back to clock in. But when I turn the corner, there's a small group of people, Shari and Es included, holding a Chocolate Suicide Cake alight with candles. They begin to sing a morbid happy birthday song about death and then they laugh uproariously and someone smacks me on the butt as I lean in to blow out the candles.

Shari hugs me. "Happy Birthday, girl. You didn't have to come in today."

I hug her back. "Yes I did. But thank you."

Es hugs me next, her tall body dwarfing me. She was a tall man once upon a time, and makes an even taller woman, given social stereotypes. But she is all woman, and one of my best friends in the world. Being transgender in a binary world can't be easy, and every day I admire the courage it takes for her to just be herself. Maybe that's why we became best friends almost instantly the day I started working here, because in our own way, we each feel this disconnect to the life we were born into. I have tears in my eyes when I look up at her. "You should have warned me," I chide.

"Neva'!" she says, a twinkle in her brown eyes as she flips her blond hair out of her face.

Shari hands me a slice of cake. "Eat up. The customers can wait."

As if on cue, someone from the bar raises his voice, complaining about the service. "What's taking so damn long? What are you all doing back there, twiddling your thumbs?"

Shari's face hardens as she storms out to give that customer a piece of her mind. "I'm sorry. I didn't realize we were married in a past life."

It's a line she uses a lot. Sometimes it works, shifting the mood into happy. When it doesn't, the customer is kicked out, blacklisted from the best diner in Portland. Their loss.

This time it works. The customer apologizes, Shari is gracious, and all is well in the world of The Roxy.

I love it here. It's my family. My second home. I've lived alone with my mother my whole life. My father died when I was a toddler and we have no other relatives. Death, disease, life…has stolen them all. It's only here, at The Roxy, that I have any real family to call my own, outside of my mother.

I finish my cake and check in to see which tables I have. I'm ready.

The night is long, but fun. We have our regulars, the guy who almost never speaks, wears the same thing every day, but always leaves a nice tip and is kind to us all, the drag queen who likes to flirt with our cook, those coming off their shifts at other bars, who are too sober and properly dressed to be out drinking all night...I greet them by name, serve them what they love most, sass them just enough to make them feel like family, like this is their place too, because it is.

But when he walks in, it's like time stands still. He's not a regular. He's never been here before. I don't know how I know this, but I know he's here for me. And my hands shake when I walk up to him, sitting in a booth alone, not looking at his menu. He has hair dark as night and eyes like the moon and sea. His skin is pale and perfect and he looks as if he's been carved from marble. He wears a tailored suit too perfect to be purchased off the rack. We get all kinds at The Roxy, but not his kind. He has no kind.

And he makes me nervous.

"What can I get you?" I ask, my tongue tripping over itself.

He looks up at me and smiles. "Are you on the menu?"

...

This is not the first time I've been hit on at The Roxy. It's a regular occurrence. They flirt, I flirt, or I sass, depending on my mood. What I don't do, what I never do, is stutter.

Until now.

I literally stutter. My armpits are sweating, my head feels hot and I might have a sudden fever. I also might vomit. What is wrong with me? Is Insta-flu a thing? Because if it is, I've clearly contracted it.

He looks amused. "Are you all right?" His voice is rich and he's got the sexiest accent, something of a cross between British and South African. He holds up his glass of water to me, his long slender fingers so perfectly manicured. "Drink."

I take the glass, and our hands touch. A chill runs through my body and I nearly drop the glass. What am I doing? I can't drink a customer's water. I put it back on the table. "I'm fine. Just...hot."

"Indeed," he says, his lips in a smirk, eyes twinkling.

"Have you...uh...decided on your...what you want?" Shut up, Ari. You sound like an idiot.

He grins, a dimple forming on his chin. "What do you recommend?"

"Depends," I say, slowing my breathing so I don't pass out. "Are you in the mood for savory or sweet?"

Everything I say suddenly feels like a double entendre with this man.

"Surprise me." He hands me his menu and tugs at the cuff of his suit.

"You don't look like a man who usually likes surprises," I say, studying him more closely as I regain my composure.

He raises a perfectly formed eyebrow at me. "Really? What kind of man do I look like?"

"A proud man who likes control."

There's a flash of surprise on his face, before his mask falls back into place. How do I know that's a mask? How do I know these things about him? I have no idea. I'm pretty intuitive about people, but I leave the fortune telling to Es's boyfriend, Pete. He's got the gift, or so everyone says. I've always been too chicken to have him read me.

Unlike this man before me, I like surprises. Life is too bleak without them.

"The way you dress," I say.

He raises an eyebrow.

"You wear an expensively tailored Italian suit into a diner. Your nails are manicured. Your skin is well-cared for. Everything about how you present yourself screams control. Precision. There's nothing that indicates you like spontaneity or surprises."

He doesn't reply, just stares into my eyes for far too long. I look around for an escape from his penetrative gaze. My eyes fall to the table, to his elegant hands. His jacket cuff is pulled up, exposing a strange kind of scar or tattoo on his wrist. "Does that mean something special?" I ask, pointing to it.

He looks down, and quickly pulls his jacket to cover it. "Just a birthmark."

I flush and look away. "I'll just…find something for you to eat." I rush off, and hide in the back until I can slow my wild heart.

Es rushes by, hands full of plates, but she pauses when she sees me. "What's the matter with you, darlin'? You're not coming down with that flu that's going around, are you? Vomit is not a good look on me."

I shake my head. "I'm not sick. Just…flustered. I don't know. It's weird. I'm fine."

She raises a plucked eyebrow at me, then glances out to my table. "Oh, I see. Darlin', that man is a gift from the Universe. He is your birthday present, all wrapped up in silk and satin. You must give him your number!"

"No way. Definitely not my type."

"Really? Tall, dark, and sexy as sin isn't your type? Pray tell what is?" She leans closer to me, and I can smell her expensive perfume. "Look, honey. You are the closest thing to a virgin The Roxy has ever seen over the age of sixteen. You need to get some before you shrivel up."

I puff out my chest in mock offense. "I am not a virgin!"

She rolls her eyes. "High school boys behind the bleachers do not count. Now get that man something delicious to eat, and I'm not talking about anything from our menu."

Despite my bold words, I blush, because she's not wrong. For a waitress at The Roxy, I'm woefully inexperienced when it comes to men.

But right now, time is ticking, my other tables are filling up, and I need to figure out what to feed this strange man, when my eyes land on my birthday cake. I cut a slice and bring it out to him. His eyes crinkle when he sees it. "Good choice," he says.

"It's my birthday cake," I spurt out. Because I'm a five-year-old with her first kindergarten crush, apparently.

"Happy birthday," he says, taking a big bite out of the cake. "My brother would love this place. Just decadent enough for him."

"You don't enjoy decadence?" I ask.

"I prefer to stay on task, to not get distracted by temporary pleasures. What about you, Arianna? What do you enjoy?"

I narrow my eyes. "How do you know my name?" We don't wear name tags at The Roxy.

"I heard your coworker mention it," he says without pause. "But you didn't answer my question. What do you enjoy?"

"Customers who tip big," I say, turning on my heel to walk away. I hear him chuckle as I stop to take the order of my next table.

When I come back, he's gone, only one bite missing from his cake. But he left a stack of twenty-dollar bills under the water glass, with a business card. I stare at it in disbelief, then count it quickly. Three hundred dollars? For a slice of cake? My breath hitches. Was this on purpose? Who is this guy? I pick up the card and study it. It's heavy card stock with engraved silver writing. No name, just a phone number and a hand-written note that says, "See you soon," in a formal cursive style in thick black ink. I stick the card and money in my pocket as a drunken man across the diner kicks the juke box.

Es deals with him, explaining with hand on hip the appropriate Roxy behavior. I catch her eye and gesture to the back, then escape the customers.

She finds me hovering over the remains of my birthday cake, staring at the money.

"Oh my! Did that sexy thing leave that for you?"

I nod, still unable to speak.

"And did you give him your number? Tell me you gave him your number!"

I shake my head. "But he gave me his." I show her the card.

She whistles under her breath. "Girlfriend, you had better call him. If you don't, I will."

I peel off a few twenties and slip them in Es's hand. "For your fund."

Her eyes fill with tears and she sniffs as she delicately brushes them away. "What are you doing, girl? Do you know how long it takes me to do my face? You can't give me this. You need it too much."

I shake my head. "Es, you've been saving for your gender reassignment surgery for years. I'm just doing my small part to help. You'll get there." She's on the hormones and she had the breast augmentation done, but there's one last piece to her transition that she hasn't been able to afford yet, and she's desperate to.

She hugs me, then flits away, mumbling about reapplying her mascara. I smile, and pick up an order for one of my tables.

The rest of my shift flies by, and my feet and back are sore when morning breaks. Es kisses my cheek and slips a small box into my hand as I leave. "Happy Birthday," she says.

I thank her and open the box. Inside is a pendant on a silver chain. The stone is beautiful—a blend of greens and blues. I slip it over my head.

"Pete said you'd need it. It's labradorite. It's protection against psychic vampirism, and it will help awaken your own powers."

I don't buy into most of that stuff, but I keep the pendant on as I walk back to my apartment. There's ice on the ground, the rain freezing in the dropping temperatures. I'm careful as I walk, and I pull my thin jacket around my body, trying to stay a little dry. It doesn't work. I'll need to budget for a new winter coat soon. I remember the wad of cash in my pocket and smile despite the cold.

I'm halfway home when once again I feel the presence of someone following me. This time, I don't try to run. Instead, I turn, pepper spray in hand, and challenge my invisible stalker. "Who's there? What do you want?"

I wait, my legs shoulder-width apart, fighting stance ready. I hear nothing, see nothing. Feeling foolish, I retrace my steps, but it's misty and I can't see much. "I know you're there!"

My voice sounds so loud, so crass in the silent, predawn morning.

Still, nothing.

I sigh and turn, walking briskly to my apartment.

The rest of the world will be waking up for their weekend soon, but my eyes are heavy, and I'm ready for bed. Then I remember I promised my mom we'd get something to eat. I yawn, stretch and try to wake myself up as I open the door. "Mom! I'm home. I'm just going to shower and change and then we can go out."

I hurry upstairs and slip out of my work clothes. My shower is quick, and I pull on my jeans and a blue sweater and use make-up to make myself look a little less tired before I see my mom. She's always worried I'm working too hard and not getting enough sleep. She's not wrong, but I can't let her know that.

I expect to find her in the living room or kitchen. When I don't, I knock on her bedroom door, the only room left besides our shared bathroom. There's no answer.

"Mom?"

I nudge the door open and peek in. I see her small foot hanging off her bed, so I push the door open all the way. She must not have woken yet.

"Mom?" I creep closer, not sure if I should wake her or let her sleep. She's lying on her back, her head turned away from me, the blankets askew around her. I can only see the back of her head, and my heart beats harder, as if it knows something I don't.

My voice becomes more panicked. "Mom!" I reach for her, my hand landing on her shoulder. She doesn't move. I brush the long hair out of her face. Her eyes are closed, but still she doesn't respond. I scream for her, but her body is motionless. Lifeless.

I reach for my cell phone and dial 9-1-1. "Please help me. I think something happened to my mother. I think she's dead."

2

THE HOSPITAL

"Sometimes wolves come in sheep's clothing."

—Fenris Vane

The medics found a pulse when they arrived, and we made fast time to the hospital in the ambulance. Now I sit, waiting. They've taken her to a private room, hooked her to machines, stuck needles in her to take her blood. They asked me to leave, to wait in the lobby and some-one would come with an update soon. They threw words around like stroke, heart attack, brain aneurysm, but no one seems to know anything. Their words are like bubbles popping in the air. No substance, just ideas.

Shoulders slumped, head pounding, I followed their orders, too tired to argue. Too heartbroken to fight anyone.

That was an hour ago. I'm still waiting. Exhausted. Terrified. The fear burns in my blood like a fever, infecting every part of me with this deepening dread of what is to come.

My phone buzzes and I look down at it. I'd forgotten I was still holding it. It's Es, texting me.

I know ur prob exhausted but want to party for ur bday?

My finger hovers over the letters trying to think of how to respond. I decide with the truth.

Mom in hospital. It's bad. Can't leave.

Her reply is instant.

Pete & I will be right there. Xo

I don't really want company, but it's also a relief to know I won't be alone for this. I wander the hospital halls looking for a coffee machine. When I find it, I realize I have no money on me. I left the house with nothing. I lean my head against the machine, an overwhelming sense of hopelessness crashing into me. It is the final straw that breaks the composure I've been clinging to this whole time. My breath hitches, the tears are threatening my eyes, but if I start crying right now, I might not stop. I try to hold it in, but a sob escapes my body, like a punch to my gut has forced it out. My fingers grip the cold metal of the coffee machine as I fight to control my emotions.

"The coffee here really isn't that good. You can do better."

The voice behind me is male, deep and gravelly and British, and I turn, embarrassed that I've been caught in such a public display of grief. I swipe at my eyes with the cuff of my sweatshirt and suck in my pain, trying to mask it in the presence of this stranger.

The man before me is tall, with lean muscles that bulge through the black jeans and black cotton shirt he wears under his long black trench coat. His hair is slightly too long and disheveled, brown with copper highlights that accent his blue eyes. His face looks carved from rock, and even as he smiles, there's a hardness to him that makes me take a step back. He could be a Greek god, and he pulses with some kind of feral energy, like a wild animal. He looks out of place in this sterile hospital environment. Like a wolf prowling amongst the sheep.

"I apologize," he says, taking a step back. "I didn't mean to frighten you."

I try to smile, but I think it comes out as more of a grimace. "You didn't. I'm just...my mom is here and...I haven't slept in a long time. I guess I needed the coffee more than I realized." I'm babbling, and I bite my tongue to shut myself up. I move away from the machine when I realize he's probably waiting on his turn to get a cup.

He puts a paper cup into the tray, sticks some change into the money slot, then presses a button. Black java pours out. He hands the cup to me when it's full. "You need this more than I do, I think."

"Oh, I can't take your coffee."

He sticks another dollar in. "I've got change for two."

He holds out his hand. It's large and callused with a few scars. "I'm Fen," he says, waiting.

"Ari." I extend my hand and when our skin touches a shiver runs up my spine.

"What happened to your mom?"

I give him a quick version of my morning, wondering why I'm telling this stranger anything.

His face is stoic, serious, when I finish. "I'm sorry about your mother. I…" He looks hesitant to speak. "I lost my father recently. It's never easy."

While I empathize with his grief, his words prick me. "My mother isn't dead. She'll get through this. But…" I pause, realizing I sound like a jerk. "I'm sorry about your father. That's awful. Is that why you're here?"

"No. I'm here on other business."

Something about his tone makes me think there's more to his story. "Do you work here?"

"I'm an independent contractor," he says. "Personal security." He looks like he wants to say more, like he has something terrible and dark he needs to share, but he shakes his head and holds up his coffee. "Take care of yourself, Ari. And be careful. Sometimes wolves come in sheep's clothing."

He turns to walk away, and I watch until he disappears around a corner, puzzling at his odd warning. What does that even mean? And how uncanny that he brought up wolves and sheep when that's exactly what I was thinking about him. I can still feel the heat of his hand against mine, the strength that pulsed through him. I'm lost in thoughts as I zombie-walk back into the waiting room and sink into a chair in the corner to continue my purgatory of waiting. The coffee is awful, but I drink it anyway, hoping it gives my muddled mind some clarity. When Es and Pete walk in carrying a bag from Painted Lady Coffee House, I stand to hug them both. "Thank you for coming."

Pete kisses my cheek. "We didn't just come. We brought provisions." He looks around the hospital, his nose crinkling with distaste. "I hope you haven't touched anything or anyone here."

I chuckle. "Of course not. I've been floating around to avoid the germs."

Es hands me a bag and a steaming cup of coffee. "Eat. Drink. You'll need your strength."

They each flank me as we sit. I sip at the coffee and sigh. "Best in Portland."

"Any news?" Pete asks. He's a short man with curly red hair and glasses. He looks as if he could have been cast as one of the Weasley's in the Harry Potter movies. There are a lot of raised eyebrows when he and Es are together in public, but they don't seem to care. Pete told me he was once beat up for being gay. "I'm not gay," he said. "Es isn't a man, she's a woman. But it really doesn't matter. I love her as she is, whatever that body is. People can be so restrictive when it comes to love, but where's the sense in that?"

I think I fell in love with Pete a little bit that day. After time, he joined the ranks of people I love the most in the world. I tell them I know nothing, that I'm still waiting for the doctor to come update me.

"I texted The Roxy," Es says. "You're off the hook for work for as long as you need."

I half smile at her, my heart sinking further as the full ramifications of today hit me. My mother won't be able to work. I'll need to take care of her. We're barely surviving as it is. How am I going to get through this? But I can't worry about that now. First, I just need to make sure my mom is okay. We'll deal with the rest later.

Pete takes the bag from my hands and pulls out a sandwich. "Your favorite. Grilled cheese with bacon. Eat some."

He waves the sandwich around like I'm a toddler he has to coerce to eat, so I take a bite. It looks amazing, but today it tastes like ash in my mouth, and I feel like vomiting. I force the food down my throat and take another drink of the coffee. "I appreciate it, but I can't eat right now. Not until I know she's all right."

He nods and puts the remains of the sandwich back in his bag. And we wait. In silence. A television stuck on daytime talk shows plays in the background as my friends offer their support.

Finally a doctor comes out and calls my name. I leap up, making myself dizzy, and speed walk toward her. She's an older woman with long graying hair pulled back into a bun.

"Hello, Miss Spero, I'm Dr. Cameron. I'm sorry you've had to wait so long."

"How is my mother?" I ask.

"It's a complicated situation," she says, looking down at a file in her hands. "Your mother has a history of using pain medication? She was injured in a car accident years ago, yes?"

My body breaks out in a cold sweat at memories that can't possibly be mine, but feel viscerally mine none-the-less. I smell the burning flesh. Hear the crash of metal on metal. Taste the smoke and blood in my mouth. "Yes, she was injured badly."

The doctor nods. "Her blood tests revealed high levels of narcotics in her system. Was she abusing her pain medication?"

"She was in a lot of pain. It was getting worse. But she wasn't abusing anything, and I don't see what this has to do with her current condition."

"Maybe it doesn't," the doctor says. "I'm just trying to understand her medical history."

"And I'm trying to understand what's wrong with her. How does a relatively healthy woman collapse like this with no provocation? What happened?"

"Your mother is in a coma," Dr. Cameron says. "Beyond that, she's essentially brain dead. Her body is functioning, but barely. Without life support she wouldn't be alive right now. And with it...I'm afraid she's only here in body. You'll have to make a difficult choice."

My knees buckle and Es and Pete catch me before I fall. I'm shaking, my muscles wobbling under the pressure of the air around me. "Are you saying I have to decide whether to pull the plug on my own mother?"

She hands me a stack of papers. "These forms explain your options, and someone from billing will come by to help you with the insurance and expenses of your choices. I'm so sorry for your loss, Miss Spero."

"I want to see her. I want to see my mother."

The doctor nods. "I'll have a nurse escort you to her room." She leaves me there alone, presumably to find a nurse, and Pete puts an arm around my shoulder. "Doctors don't know everything," he says.

"What do you mean?"

He looks at me, an unreadable expression on his face. "There are a lot of studies of people in comas. A lot of evidence to suggest they are aware and hear us. Some even have memories of conversations when they finally wake up."

"She said my mother is brain dead." The words sink like rocks in my throat, choking me.

"There's a lot science can't explain. Don't give up hope."

"Hope. Did you know that's what my last name means? Spero is hope in Latin. My mom always says it's a reminder to never lose hope, no matter how bleak the situation. *Dum spiro spero.*"

"'While I breathe, I hope,'" he says, surprising me with the English translation of the Latin.

I nod. "That's what she'd tell me."

"It's good to have hope," he says.

A nurse arrives to take me back.

Es and Pete follow at my heels but the nurse shakes his head. "I'm sorry, only family is permitted beyond this point."

Es squeezes my hand. "We'll be here waiting for you, honey. Take as long as you need."

I nod and follow the nurse through the halls and around a corner. He stops in front of a door and pauses, his hand on the latch. "We've made her as comfortable as possible."

"Thank you."

He opens the door, and I walk in with determination. I won't give up. I won't stop believing she is in there somewhere. She's still breathing. There's still hope.

My mom is lying in the bed, hooked up to machines and monitors, when we walk in. Her skin is pale, her face blank, expressionless, her red, wild hair spread over her pillow. I walk over and reach for her hand, holding it, praying for some sign that she can hear me. "Hi, Mom. It's Ari. I'm here now, and everything is going to be okay."

The nurse checks my mother's chart then walks to the door. "I'll leave you alone with her. Ring the buzzer if you need anything."

"What's your name?" I ask, as he's about to leave.

"I'm Tom, and I'll be on shift the rest of the day. I'll take good care of your mother."

"Thank you, Tom."

I look back at my mom and smooth the hair out of her eyes. "I need you. You can't leave me yet. I may be an adult, but I still need you." I squeeze her hand, turning it over in mine, and I notice something on the inside of her wrist. A design I've never seen before. A sort of stylized number seven with two lines parallel to the top. It's not a tattoo, or a burn. It almost looks…like a scar, but not really. It's raised and pale, almost glowing. Just like the symbol on the stranger at The Roxy last night. Well, the actual design is different, but the style, the strangeness of it is the same. I take my phone out and snap a picture, then text it to Es and Pete.

Either of you seen something like this?

Pete texts back first.

Need to talk ASAP!

I frown at his response.

Do you know something about this symbol?

He doesn't respond. I tap on the screen of my phone, as if that will make him respond faster. When it doesn't, I sigh and look at my mom. She's so still. I want to believe. To have hope.

I'm about to leave, to seek out Pete and find out what he knows, when a petite woman in a business suit walks in with a clipboard. "Miss Spero, I need to get some information about your mother's insurance."

I can't believe I have to deal with the banality of money and insurance when my mother is fighting for her life, and thirty minutes later I want to scream. Her insurance won't cover even a fraction of what it would take to keep her on life support long term. And the cost. All those zeros. I can't even begin to fathom how I'll come up with the money.

All on the hope that she might someday wake up.

I take the papers the woman hands me and stand. "I'll have to think about this," I say, skirting out the door.

I find Es and Pete snuggling in the waiting room watching cat videos on Pete's phone. When they see me they both stand. "We need to talk," Pete says.

I nod.

Pete looks around like someone might be watching. Like anyone cares at all about our conversation. "But not here."

I roll my eyes and follow him out of the hospital. He's parked out front.

I freeze. "Why don't we just walk?"

Es reaches for my hand. "It's time, darlin'. You have to get over this."

Today? Do I really have to do this today? But as I'm standing there, a torrent of rain falls from the sky, soaking us all. To their credit, my friends stand there in the rain, soaking wet, cold, shivering, waiting for me. I nod and climb into the back of the car. "Where are we going?"

"Your house should be safe enough. If that's okay? Our roommate is home and not to be trusted with this conversation," Pete says, pulling out onto the street.

"How are things going with the roommate?" I ask, bracing my hands against the back of Pete's seat, my knuckles turning white.

Es looks over her shoulder at me, rolling her eyes. "It's a nightmare. I swear to god, once I have the money for my surgery, we are out of there." She reaches for Pete's free hand. "It's time we had our own place."

The roads are slick with ice and Pete drives like an old woman, for which I'm grateful. My nails leave imprints in the faux-leather fabric, and I don't stop shaking until we pull up in front of my apartment. When I slide out of the car, I'm dizzy with the jagged memories that cut at me like broken glass.

Es and Pete wait patiently as I take several deep breaths. When I feel like I can walk without falling, I nod and lead them to the door, which is still unlocked; no one would want to steal anything we have. Still, I lock it behind me as we all enter.

Es heads straight to the heater, to turn it on.

"Sorry, it's busted," I tell her. "We'll have to stay bundled."

She smiles. "Don't you worry a thing about it. How's about I make us all some hot coffee and we can sit down and figure this out together."

Es heads to my small kitchen, and I sink into the couch in the living room. Suddenly my whole body aches, and I feel the hours of sleepless exhaustion take its toll on me, but I'm too wired to actually sleep. The apartment is too still. Too quiet. Even the annoying hum of the refrigerator is missing, and I idly wonder if it stopped working as well. There are small signs of my mother everywhere. Her boots by the front door, one lying on its side. Her jacket draped over the back of one of the kitchen chairs. Her favorite magazines spread out on the table in front of the couch.

Pete sits in the love seat across from me, and Es brings us coffees and sits next to him.

Now that we are all settled, I lean in to Pete. "Okay, spill it."

Pete pulls out his phone to look at the picture I sent. "Whose wrist is this?"

"My mom's."

He frowns. "How long has she had a mark like this?"

"It's new," I say. "I've never seen it until today."

"So it wasn't there before she fell into this coma?" he asks.

"No."

"This is bad, Ari. Very bad."

I blow on my coffee and sip it, trying to control my impatience. "Enough with the scary omens. Just tell me."

He opens up a browser on his phone and shows me image after image of the mark on my mom's wrist.

"This is the Mark of Cain. You know the story of Cain and Abel? From the Bible?"

I nod, recalling old Bible stories from my childhood. An old neighbor of ours used to babysit me when I was little and my mom was working. She'd drag me to church with her, and was devoted to the idea that my soul needed saving. It didn't stick, but I remember some of it. "They were both told by God to make sacrifices to him, or something. Abel's was accepted by God but Cain's was rejected. He and Abel fought and Cain killed his brother and was marked for it."

"That's the gist. But some believe there's more to the story. Some believe that mark did more than just serve as a sign to others that he deserved death. Some believe that mark turned him."

"Turned him into what?" I ask.

"Into a demon. One who feeds on the pain of others. That he was condemned to spend eternity torturing others or he would feel that torture himself, day in and day out for all time."

I shake my head. "This is why religion does not make sense to me. What kind of God asks for blood sacrifices, then punishes people who don't do it?"

"A vengeful God," Pete says.

"So what does this have to do with my mother?" I shudder, feeling an evil premonition descend upon me.

"If she bears the Mark of Cain, then she is his." Pete whispers this so quietly it takes my mind a moment to make sense of his words.

"You think my mom is being held prisoner by Cain—a demon?"

He doesn't answer, but I can see on his face that's exactly what he believes. I look to Es for help. Surely she can't believe this nonsense? But she averts her eyes, her shoulders slumped, her hand resting on Pete's knee. She believes him.

"Have you both lost your mind? These stories aren't real. It's all just a bunch of morality tales meant to scare kids—and adults—into behaving in the way whoever was in charge wanted them to."

Pete shakes his head. "I know you're a skeptic, and I've never tried to push my beliefs on you, but Ari...you have to open your eyes. There are things in this world that defy logic."

I want to argue, to tell him there's a very logical and rational explanation for what happened to my mother, to tell him I will find a way to save her with science. But I can't. My mind returns to the man at The Roxy. The man with the same kind of mark but in a different design. The man with the strange eyes and the accent

I couldn't place. The man who knew my name, my full name, when no one at work calls me Arianna only Ari.

"I have to go!" I say, jumping up. "I need to see my mom again."

Pete drives me to the hospital, and in the urgency to see my mother again, I tolerate being in the car with less terror than normal. Yay for me. When we arrive, Pete tries to park, but I tell him and Es to go home and rest. "I need some time to process things, and you both need sleep. I'll call you later, okay?"

They relent and drive off, leaving me in drifts of newly fallen snow at the front door of the hospital. The sun has already set, marking the end of a day that has seemed an eternity. I run in and find my mother's room. She's still lying there, just as she was. I turn her wrist over and stare at the mark. Is this really the Mark of Cain? Could the story be true?

I pull out the strange man's business card and dial the number on it.

"I was expecting your call, though I admit, I thought it would arrive earlier," he says before I've even have a chance to speak.

"Who are you? What have you done to my mother?"

"I've done nothing to your mother. But without me, she will be lost for good. Without me, her soul will suffer for all eternity." His voice echoes around me, and I look up to see him standing at the door of my mother's room, holding his phone to his ear.

When he sees me notice him, he smiles and puts his phone away. "Hello Arianna Spero. It's time at last we talked. Tell me, do you want to save your mother?"

3

STRANGER DANGER

"Let's put the blame where it belongs, shall we?"
—Arianna Spero

My phone goes dead, so I stick it back into my pocket and stare at the man in front of me. He's dressed as impeccably today as he was yesterday—a tailored Italian suit, this time in grey and silver, with a leather brief-case hanging at his side. Was it just yesterday that he came in to The Roxy? It seems so long ago now.

But this time I'm not daunted by his perfection, by his beauty, by the sheer *otherness* of him. This time I'm just pissed. I march over to him and slap his face. Hard.

He rubs his jaw, though I have the distinct impression that my palm hurts a lot more than his cheek.

I shake out the pain in my hand as discreetly as I can. "Tell me what's going on before I have you arrested."

His eyes widen in surprise, but he looks more amused than angry. "You really aren't what I expected."

I glare at him, my fists on my hips. "Why were you expecting anything at all? Who are you?" My jaw hurts from gritting my teeth.

"You can call me Asher, and I'm the only one who can save your mother. With your help."

I glance at her still form lying in the hospital bed. "What's wrong with her?"

"Your friend was right, mostly. She bears the Mark of Cain and is in a hell dimension for all eternity." He speaks glibly, as if this is all just a joke to him.

I step back and frown. "Right. Of course. That makes perfect sense. Mark of Cain. Hell dimension. Demons. What happens next?" I hold up a hand before he can speak. "No wait, let me guess. You tell me I'm some kind of chosen one and in exchange for my soul or some such nonsense you will save my mom. There's probably a prophecy involved, and some danger, and you think your sexy charms will overcome all that and sway me to your way of thinking, yes? Sorry, dude. I've seen that movie."

He tries to speak, but his mouth just kind of hangs open, no sound coming out. He has a look of confusion on his face, but he recovers quickly, snapping his mouth closed and staring at me, his eyes unreadable. "What are you?"

"What am I? Are you seriously asking me that? After everything you just tried to sell me?"

His eyes dart around the room and land on my mother. "You have an uncanny way of seeing to the truth of things," he says. He returns his gaze to me. "Be that as it may, you aren't entirely wrong. Your mother's soul is trapped. You are her only hope. And..." he steps closer to me and grins..."I'm glad you at least think I'm sexy."

Now it's my turn to stare gape-mouthed. "I never..."

He winks at me. "You did. You accused me of having 'sexy charms.' Close enough. So, now that we are on the same page, let us get to the crux of this shall we?"

I cross my arms over my chest. "What is the crux of this? What do you want from me?"

"Your soul, of course."

I roll my eyes. "You evil guys should come up with better lines."

He pulls a scroll out of a briefcase and hands it to me. "This is what I want from you, in exchange for your mother's soul."

I unroll the beige, ancient-looking parchment. It's so old I fear it will disintegrate in my hands, the paper crinkled and webbed. It even smells old, like ink and ancient castles from books. I begin to read. It takes me a while, the font is some kind of calligraphy that doesn't exactly encourage skimming. He could stand to learn about font choices and their impact on reading.

When I'm done, I roll it up and shove it back at him. "Am I being tricked?"

He looks down at the scroll in his hand in confusion. "What?"

"Tricked? Or something? Is there some new reality show I'm the star of? I can't imagine my mom would be a part of this, but maybe for enough money she would. Is this a joke? Some plot to make a fool of me or try to sway me to believe in God and demons and the supernatural?" I don't believe my own words. I've seen my mom, and she's well and truly missing from her body, but none of this makes sense. I feel trapped in some surreal alternate reality where nothing is right. Everything is wrong. This is wrong.

"I do not know what you mean by 'reality show' but I can assure you I would never associate myself with such a crass sounding thing. This is deadly real."

My bravado is fading, because he doesn't look like the kind of man who plays pranks, and my mom doesn't look like she's faking a coma, and this hospital is entirely too real. I point to the paper in his hand. "That says my mom made a deal with a devil, that she traded her soul, and now the only way I can free her is to give you...me."

The man nods. "My brothers and I...we are in a bit of a predicament, and you are our only hope." He smiles as if he knows what that word means to me.

"And who are you and your brothers?" I look around for the cameras, for some evidence I'm being pranked. Maybe this guy escaped from the psych ward. That would explain a lot.

"Have you not figured it out yet?" His eyes change colors, becoming brighter. "We are the Princes of Hell. And you will be a Princess to one of us, and ultimately, Queen."

"Of hell," I say.

He nods. "Of hell. Though we have our own names for our world. Hell is a very mundane and human term that does not mean what you think it means."

"You're a demon."

He bows regally. "At your service."

"And this contract I would have to sign. It would be for eternity?"

"Yes."

"And I would have to choose one of you to marry?"

"Yes."

I look down at the scroll still in my hand. "And give that prince an heir."

"Correct."

"What happens after I die? In, say, seventy years?"

He chuckles. "Do you not understand? You will never die. By agreeing to this, you agree to take the Blood Oath. You will become one of us."

"One of you? You mean a demon. I would have to become a demon."

"In a manner of speaking, yes."

My stomach quivers with raw nerves at his answers. "And my child? This heir I'm promising...what if I can't get pregnant? Does that negate the contract?"

He steps forward and raises his hand to my cheek, brushing aside a strand of hair. "There will be ample opportunity to work on that. Worry not."

My hands are shaking. My throat is dry. The world no longer makes any sense. This is no longer funny. I place my hands on his chest...and push. "Get. Out."

It's like pushing a boulder. He only moves because he chooses to. I'm under no illusions about that.

"It's an interesting kind of irony that you of all people do not believe in demons." He looks darkly amused, his lips curling into a mocking smile.

When he moves again, it is with such speed I don't even register his movement until he is pressed up against me, my back now slammed against the wall. "But if you want to save your mother, I suggest you surrender your disbelief and embrace the truth. There are monsters in the world, Arianna. They are real." His eyes glow again, this time bright silver, and he smiles. "*I* am real."

I swallow, but my throat is too dry. I can't breathe.

His eyes bore into me, then drop to the throbbing vein on my neck. His eye teeth elongate until he has… fangs. His hand wraps around my neck and he lowers his mouth to my throat, his teeth brushing against my skin.

I'm shaking so hard, my breathing coming in rapid gulps. I close my eyes, waiting for…something. Death. Him to eat me. This no longer feels like a prank, but my mind can't wrap itself around the reality.

"Your mother will suffer for all eternity if you do not accept this deal," he whispers against my neck. "And I suggest you do not take too long to decide. I smell death on her. Even with those machines, she will not survive the week."

A sob builds in my throat, and I open my eyes, ready to scream, to gouge his eyes out, to do something to protect myself. But the pressure on my throat disappears and when my vision clears, I am alone in the hospital room with my mother. The stranger is gone.

But the scroll is sitting on the table by the hospital bed. Next to it is a manila folder with a note in his scrawl. *When you are ready to see reason, read this file. It will answer questions of your past. It will show you this is no trick.*

I sink to the floor, shaking, fighting tears, trying to clear my mind so I can think straight. This can't be real. These kinds of things don't exist.

Demons.

Vampires.

They don't exist.

I wipe my eyes and stand, then take a deep breath. Time to get some answers. I run out of the room and down the hall, to the admittance desk. "There was a man in my mother's room. Tall, tailored suit, dark hair, light eyes. Why was he allowed back here?"

The nurse looks at me in confusion. "No one has been back there but you and the hospital staff."

"Are you sure?" I ask, looking around frantically. "I just saw him."

"This is the only way in and out, and I've been here without a break for hours. I'm sure." She looks more closely at me. "Are you okay? Do you need a doctor? You look pale."

I snort. "I'm always pale. Thanks, anyway." I walk back to my mother's room and sit next to her bed, ignoring the files the man left. I caress her hand, my thumb running over the mark on her wrist. "What's going on, Mom? What did you do?"

...

The hospital room feels like it's closing in on me. I can smell his cologne lingering, as if he's still here, lurking, spying, waiting to pounce. I've shut my mind down for now. There's no space in my attention to consider the existence of vampires and demons. To entertain the possibility that my mother is under a curse that will entrap her soul for all eternity and kill her body.

When Tom comes in to check on her, he studies me thoughtfully. "You should get some rest, honey. We'll take good care of her."

I've been up for two days. He's right, I should sleep, but I don't know how. "What if something happens?"

"She looks stable, but we'll call if anything changes. I'm on duty all night, so I'll keep an eye out. Rest. You're no good to her if you get sick."

I nod and grab my bag. My eyes fall to the scroll and folder. I haven't looked at them yet, and I'm not ready to, but I don't want anyone else gaining access to whatever they contain, so I shove them in my bag, lean over and kiss my mom on the forehead, and then quickly leave the room.

I can't wait to escape the hospital, and when a winter storm greets me, I smile. I might freeze to death on the way home, but I love snow. I love the way the world looks when it's covered in white powder. Magical.

The sun has already set and the street lamps cast long shadows over the snowy sidewalks. My breath is white as I exhale, and I round my shoulders and hug myself to preserve what little warmth I have.

While walking through the parking lot to the sidewalk, someone calls my name. I turn and see

Fen standing by a black and silver motorcycle. He's already straddling it. "You'll catch your death out here," he says.

I shrug. "It's not so bad." Though I can barely feel my toes or my nose anymore, but whatever.

"Get on," he says, looking at the seat behind him. "I've got an extra helmet."

"Um. I can't. I don't live far. I'll be fine walking." I can feel the hives lurking under my skin at the thought of being on a motorcycle. That's even worse than a car. I take a deep breath.

He cocks his head, but instead of arguing, he takes his trench coat off and hands it to me. "If you insist on walking, at least wear appropriate clothing."

"You're wearing a t-shirt," I say. "That's less than what I'm wearing."

He chuckles. "I'm used to the cold. We get much worse where I'm from. Wear it."

I want to argue, to hand it back to him, but honestly, I'm freezing, and he's already starting his motorcycle. "Be safe, Ari."

Before I can thank him or say goodbye, he's gone. I look down at the trench coat and then pull it on. It's warmed by his body heat and smells like him, a musky woodsy scent that makes me think of tall trees and wind. I luxuriate in the thick wool as it falls to my feet, bringing warmth back into my body.

The walk home is a lot more pleasant now that I'm not freezing to death. I'm lost in thought, enjoying the feeling of the snow crunching under my feet as I walk the familiar path home, when something makes me stop.

It's not a sound. Not really. More that sense of impending doom. Someone is following me again. Is it the man from the hospital? The...I can't even bring myself to call him what I saw him to be. I just need to keep calm and get home. I'll be safe there.

Maybe it's just my imagination playing tricks on me. I haven't slept in so long, I'm probably starting to hallucinate or something. Maybe it's nothing.

But as I walk past the alley next to my apartment unit, someone grabs me and pulls me into the shadows.

I try to scream but a hand covers my mouth. "This will go better for you if you stop fighting."

I bite the hand and hear the man curse, but he doesn't let go. My eyes search around frantically for a way out, for a weapon, for anything. But all I see are two more people dressed in black approaching me. Winter masks cover their faces, and I know they are here for me.

One of them pulls out a needle.

Why not a gun? I slump in my attackers arms and slam the heel of my shoe into his knee. His grip loosens, and I spin in his arms and bring my knee up to make contact with his groin. He slumps over in pain, but it doesn't stop him from pulling me back.

I'm waiting for the others to attack me, but they are distracted by something else. No, someone else.

The two in black are thrown aside like dolls, and I feel the needle jab into my neck just as my eyes lock onto the person who attacked them.

Recognition dawns just as my consciousness fades.

...

My head is pounding and my mouth feels like someone filled it with cotton balls and told me to swallow. I try to keep my breathing steady, and I keep my eyes closed. I don't know where I am yet, and I don't want my captors to know I'm awake.

Why am I even still alive? No good reason, I'm sure.

I don't hear anything at first, but then small sounds trickle in. Someone is in the room with me, pacing. They have heavy boots that aren't muffled by the carpeting. I'm laying on something lumpy and made of corduroy. Something I recognize.

I listen more closely and I hear it: the faint hum of my refrigerator. It started working again. I'm on my couch.

A phone rings and a man answers with a deep, gravelly, British voice. "I have her. She's safe."

Pause.

"No, I do not."

Pause.

"There were three of them and my priority was pro-tecting the girl."

Pause.

"Very well."

He stops talking, and I wait a few moments before I take a deep breath as if just waking up. I try to open my eyes next.

Big mistake.

Light *hurts*.

I moan, raising my hand to shield my face.

The lights go out and someone walks closer to me. "Do not move too quickly. You are still recovering from the sedative they gave you."

Large hands hold my back and head and help me into a sitting position. When I finally pry my eyes open, I look up and see the man who rescued me from my attackers.

Fen.

"What happened?" I ask, rubbing my head.

He hands me a glass of water and sits across from me. "You were attacked. I intervened and brought you home. The effects of the sedative should wear off soon. You'll feel tired and out of sorts but you will be fine."

I reach up to rub the spot on my neck where the needle entered me. It's covered in a bandage. "Thank you." As my brain wakes up, I have so many questions, but I start with the most obvious ones. "Who are you? And how is it you happened to be around when I was attacked?"

"My name is Fenris Vane. My friends call me Fen. When I saw you leave the hospital to walk home alone, I worried something might happen."

I narrow my eyes at him. "Really? Did you see someone following me? Why do you even care what happens to a random stranger?"

"Stick to being grateful, girl. Asking questions only leads to trouble."

"It appears I'm in trouble no matter what I do. First my mom mysteriously falls into a coma, and now I'm being attacked and drugged. And you show up, all rugged and viciously protective. Does that seem like a coincidence to you?"

"It seems to me like you need to be more careful." He sits there, so arrogant, so full of himself. I just want to slap him.

"*I* need to be more careful? How about other people need to stop attacking me? How about that? Let's put the blame where it belongs, shall we?"

He sighs and stands. "You are exhausting, and I have stayed here longer than I should. I made you something to eat in the kitchen. If you start to feel nauseous or dizzy, see a doctor. And try not to get yourself killed."

He walks to the door and my heart rate spikes. Suddenly I'm terrified of being left alone. My bravado drains out of me like water from a leaky glass. "Wait."

He stops and turns to me, his hand on my doorknob.

"Don't go. Please. I'm..." I swallow, hating to admit this to anyone, let alone this man. "I'm scared." My voice cracks and a tear leaks out. "I don't know what's going on. I don't understand why anyone is trying to hurt me or my mom, and I...I don't want to be alone tonight. Will you stay?"

I can see he is battling with himself, and I'm honestly not even sure why I think this is a good idea at all. He's a stranger I know nothing about. He could rob me, kill me, rape me. But, he saved me. He took me home and looked after me until I woke up. If he was going to hurt me, he would have done it by now.

"Fine. I shall stay for a few hours, but I must leave before dawn. I have somewhere to be."

I smile and sink back into the couch, suddenly exhausted. "Thank you."

He sits down again and watches me in silence.

After a few moments, I feel entirely too self-conscious. "Want to watch a movie?"

"A movie?" he asks.

"Yes. Comedy? Romance? Drama? Action?" I reach for the remote and click the TV on, then pull out my case of DVDs. "What are you in the mood for?"

53

"Hunting," he says, under his breath.

"A movie about hunting?" I'm confused.

"Action," he clarifies. "Something with action."

"Of course. But you should try a good romance sometime. You might find you like it."

He scowls at me, and I just laugh and put in something with a lot of guns and fighting and car chases. He has to sit next to me to see the television, and so we are close, our legs and arms touching, as we watch the movie. I find it boring, and Fen honestly doesn't seem that interested either, so half way through the movie I start to ask him questions about himself. His answers are vague, and I realize he's a private man, hard to get to know.

I give up and focus back on the movie, but I'm still so tired and my eyelids become so very heavy.

When I wake up again, my head is on Fen's lap, and his large hand is on my head, fingers tangled in my hair. I can hear him breathing deeply. He's sleeping.

His leg is like a log under my head, all muscle. I smile and lay still, enjoying the sound of his breathing.

When he finally wakes, he moves me gently. "I must be off," he whispers in the dark, as he repositions a pillow under my head to take the place of his lap.

I'm still exhausted, and too tired to protest or get up, so I just watch him leave and wonder if I'll ever see this mysterious man again.

The next time I wake, I feel stronger, more rested. I stretch, use the bathroom, then head to the kitchen for food. True to his word, Fen cooked. Chicken stir fry with vegetables and rice. I heat a bowl in the microwave and sit to eat, my mind wandering to last night and everything that happened.

I take my time eating, because the next thing I have to do will be hard. I text Es and ask if she and Pete can come over. As much as I hate to admit it, I'll need a ride to the hospital later. I don't want to walk after what happened last night. Part of me thinks I should report the attack to the police, but I don't. Because as much as I don't want to admit it, this has to have something to do with vampires and demons. And how could I possibly explain that to the police?

Es and Pete arrive a few minutes later. They bring food, but I'm full and let them have at it. "Thanks for coming over. I'm going to pack a few of my mom's things to make her more comfortable at the hospital. Will you hang out?"

They agree, and I leave them downstairs as I head to my mom's room. This is the hard part.

There are clothes piled on a chair in the corner that she meant to put away. Her dresser drawer is still ajar. I walk over, running my hand over the faded faux wood until it lands on an 8x10 framed picture of my mom and dad smiling over me when I was just a baby. We all looked so happy. So free. I pick up the picture and study it, looking for hidden secrets. If what the man in the hospital said is true, how would my mom have even known how to make a bargain with a demon? None of it makes sense.

I put the picture down gently and move to her bed, which is still a slept-in mess. I can see the impressions of her body from where she was laying when I found her.

I sit on the bed and then lay my head on her pillow. It smells like her shampoo. When I close my eyes I can almost imagine she's still here, humming as she folds laundry or cleans the house.

The tears I've been fighting so hard to keep at bay finally unleash themselves, and once they start, I can't stop them. It's a tidal wave of emotion that demands its time. My heart breaks, my grief pouring out of me as I clutch her pillow and wish for a different outcome.

I'm drowning in the sea of my emotional waste when my cell phone rings. "Miss Spero, this is Tom, your mother's nurse. You need to come quickly. Your mother is showing signs of distress."

I jump up, my heart hammering. I want to ask more questions, but I can't waste time. I grab my bag and run downstairs to where Es and Pete are watching television. "Something's wrong with my mom. We have to go back to the hospital."

4

THERE'S NO PLACE LIKE HELL

"There are monsters in the world, Arianna.

They are real. I am real."

—Asher

I'm in my mom's room, watching the machines pump life into her as the doctor explains what's happening.

"Her body is failing," Dr. Cameron says. "She doesn't have much longer, I'm afraid."

"I don't understand." I walk over and hold her hand, my finger once again brushing on the strange mark on her wrist. "Why can't the machines keep her alive longer? Can't people live for years this way?"

"Some, yes," the doctor says. "But not everyone. Sometimes the damage is too great. The body too weak." She's firm, calm, so sure of herself and her diagnosis.

But I can't accept this is it. The end of her story. "How long does she have?" I ask, my voice shaking.

"Hours, at most." She glances down at my mother's chart. "Maybe less." When she looks up, her eyes are compassionate, but in a detached, doctor way. She must see death all the time. "I'm sorry. I wish there was more we could do. I'll leave you alone to say your goodbyes."

Tom, the nurse who has always been so kind to me, squeezes my hand as he follows the doctor out. "I'm sorry, honey."

Once they leave and the door is closed firmly behind them, I sink into the chair next to my mother. I'm not ready to say goodbye. Not yet. Not forever.

My eyes fall to my bag. I still have the file Asher gave me. His note said it would show me the truth. I reach for it and tear it open, spreading the papers out on the edge of my mother's bed. There are newspaper clippings and police reports. I read through them quickly, then again more slowly.

Then once more. Word by word.

Seventeen years ago a fiery car crash in Seattle, Washington claimed the lives of David Stranson and his two-year-old daughter. The mother, Camilla, survived with severe injuries. Attached to the police report are death certificates for both the father and child.

The newspaper article also features a picture of the family. A mother and father smiling over their baby.

It is the picture that freezes my blood. That stops my heart. That shortens my breath.

It is the picture my mother has on her dresser.

The picture of me with my parents.

I study each document carefully. The names are different, but everything else is the same. Dates, birthdays, physical descriptions.

I squeeze my eyes shut as my nightmares flash in my mind. Screeching metal. The smell of burning rubber. Blood everywhere. Screaming. Pain. Darkness.

"You are remembering. That is good."

My eyes pop open and land on the mysterious man—the demon...the vampire—standing on the other side of my mother's bed. "What is this?" I stand and hold the papers in my fist. "How could any of this be true?"

"I have already told you," Asher says, his voice smooth, polished, hypnotic. "You died that day in the accident. Your mother made a deal, her soul to save your life. She was smart. She bargained for more time, time to raise you to adulthood. Then her payment came due, and deals made with devils cannot be broken."

My hand is shaking as I drop the paperwork onto the bed and collapse in the chair. "So it's all true? This is real?"

"It is. And you must decide soon, if you want to save her life." He looks pointedly at my mother. As if on cue, her monitor begins to beep.

"Did you do that?" I ask.

"No. Her body is failing. Make your choice, Arianna. Sign in blood and let this be done. The moment you do, she will stabilize."

I pick up the paperwork and shove it into my bag before the hospital staff come to check on the monitors. "And your contract guarantees her physical safety until her soul is returned to her?" I ask as I pull my bag to me. "She will not die by any means? She will return to her body in full health?"

"As you wish," he says.

I pull the scroll out of my bag and hand it to him. "Write that in. Include that specifically. That she will be restored to full and perfect health when she awakens. That she will not die or be harmed while she is in the coma. That you will make sure she has the best medical care and that all her bills will be covered."

He raises an eyebrow. "Very well." Pulling out a pen, he adds a few lines in neat scroll to the contract.

My mind is spinning. My mother is dying. I have to hurry, but once I sign this, it's over. I have no more room for negotiation. "Also, I want to be able to come back here for one day every week to check on my mom and see my friends."

Asher shakes his head. "You ask too much. This is not as simple as taking a drive to the town over."

I narrow my eyes at him. "You sure seem to get around fast enough when you want. It can't be that hard. I have to be able to check on my mom, to make sure you are holding up your end of the bargain. I don't know why I'm so important to your plans, and I'm sure I'll find out in some mysterious and nefarious way, but in the meantime, if you really do need me, then make this happen."

"Not every week," he says. "That is too much. Once a month. And only for half a day."

"Fine, once a month, but for a full day."

"Half a day, or nothing," he says, and I can see in his eyes I have no room left with which to negotiate. I swallow and nod.

"Very well," he grumbles, adding in my terms. He hands the scroll back to me as Tom comes in.

The monitor is still beeping, louder now. Tom looks between me and Asher. "Only family is allowed in here," he says.

"I am family," Asher says, smiling.

Tom looks to me as if to make sure this is okay. I nod and he shrugs and checks the monitors, his face paling when he sees the readouts. "I need to get the doctor. Be right back."

He scurries out, and I look down at the scroll, reading through the changes. My mother's body begins to seize and the doctor rushes in with two nurses. They tell us to get out of the way, and Asher and I fall back to give them space. He hands me a quill with a sharp edge that looks more like a knife, and leans over to whisper in my ear. "It takes blood to bind us."

I turn away from the hospital staff and place the scroll on a rolling table, then slice my arm with the quill. The cut stings and my eyes water as the pen's sharp tip soaks up the blood. I find the spot meant for my name, and with my own fresh blood, I sign.

The moment I dot the 'i' in Arianna, the machines attached to my mother fall silent. I suck in my breath as a hot flash of pain burns the inside of my right wrist. I push up the cuff of my sweatshirt and see a raised symbol forming in my flesh.

Asher flashes his own wrist. "You belong to us now," he says ominously. He takes the scroll from my hand and tucks it into his suit, then bows. "I'll give you today to wrap up your earthly affairs. Tonight you will make your new home in hell."

I look over at my mom, who is still lying in bed lifeless, but there is color in her face that wasn't there before. She looks healthier. More alive. The doctor and nurses examine her, perplexed expressions on their faces.

"Your mother has stabilized, against all odds," the doctor says. "I've never seen anything like it."

When I turn to say something to Asher, he's already gone. Instead, I go to my mother and hold her hand, feeling a sickening dread at what I've just done, but also a strange kind of hope. If she lives, if she comes back into her body restored, healed, and no longer in pain, then it was worth it.

I hope.

...

I spend the next few hours thinking of a cover story for my impending absence that won't make me sound insane. And I wonder at the logistics. Do I keep my apartment for if and when my mother heals? Pack it up? What are the social protocols for absconding to hell after making a deal with a vampire demon?

When I leave the hospital and head to The Roxy, I'm prepared, but it's still not easy when I tell them I'm resigning.

There are hugs and tears and Shari pulls me aside and stashes an envelope full of money into my bag. "Take care of yourself, girl. And don't be a stranger. Free food for life, right here."

I hug her and kiss her cheek. "Thank you."

Es is at work that day, and she hears the news first. The news being my fake story about how that rich stranger who came into The Roxy the other night offered me a high paying job with his law firm after finding out about my interest in law, but it means international travel and being gone for a long time. "It also means the best health insurance. My mom will be taken care of, and I'll be able to support her when she recovers," I explain.

Es is a sobbing mess, hugging me and making me promise to keep in touch. An idea occurs to me and I smile. "How would you and Pete like to move into my apartment while I'm gone? I know you hate your room-mate. This would give you privacy, and I need someone to look after it. You can have my room."

Her eyes light up, even through the smudged makeup. "That would be...amazing. But are you sure? It has all of your things. And your mom's..."

"I'm sure. I don't want to leave it empty while I'm gone. Take it. You'd be doing me a favor." She already has a key, so I just tell her I'm leaving that night, and I'll pack up my room so she has space for her things.

We hug again and I leave, my heart heavy from the goodbyes. Is there Wi-Fi in this hell world, I wonder? Will I ever see my mother and friends again? My con-tract negotiation skills might have gotten me what I wanted, but that doesn't mean the princes will honor it once I'm in their world. They could do anything they want to me once I'm there, and no one would ever know. My attention is drawn to the strange new mark on my wrist. I don't know if it's just my imagination, but I can almost feel the power in my skin tying me to the princes and my new life, binding me to them for all eternity. The thought that this might be the final goodbye nearly cripples me, but I can't let Es see that. I have to stay strong, just a little while longer.

I don't know what to expect, or what to bring. I pack up my room, put the boxes in my mom's, and shove a few things into my own bag to take with me. Mostly the sentimental items I can't replace, plus my favorite jeans and shirts and a sweatshirt.

My thoughts drift to Fen as I wait for Asher to arrive. I would have liked to say goodbye, but I have no way of contacting him. I tried looking for him last time I was at the hospital, to no avail. I consider leaving a note for Es to give him, just in case he pops back around while I'm gone, but what would it say? *Sorry I missed you. Living in hell now. Wish you were here?*

That probably won't work. So I just send a silent message out to him, thanking him for his help and wishing him well, wherever he might be.

I pace my living room for another hour, waiting, when finally the doorbell rings. I wasn't sure if the vampire would actually knock or just magically appear as he's wont to do.

I open the door and Asher is standing there, smiling, looking like he just stepped out of a GQ magazine. "Let's go to hell, shall we?"

. . .

I'm not ready. Not at all. But he leads me to a limousine parked in front of my apartment, and I freeze. "Can't we...I don't know...walk?"

He frowns, staring at me. "Walk? You think we can walk to where we are going?"

"Well, I don't think we can get there via limousine either," I say. "So you must be taking me someplace... human...where we will then use whatever black magic you wield to enter your world. So can't we walk to your human place at least?"

"No. Get in."

I sigh and slide in, clutching my bag to my lap as I sit awkwardly in the plush leather seats. I've never been in a limo before, but Asher looks like this is something he's quite used to.

He offers me a glass of champagne as the driver pulls out of the parking spot, but I shake my head. "I'm good, thanks."

"You look terrified. How is it that when I expose you to the monsters of nightmares, you respond with sass, but when I put you in a vehicle, you tremble with fear?" It only takes a moment for the proverbial lightbulb to go off in his head. "I see. The accident. You are still traumatized. Pity. You're much too fierce and clever to live under the weight of that one moment your whole life. You really should move on."

I snort. "Sure thing, Prince. I'll get right on that."

He scowls at me and we don't talk again for the rest of the drive. It takes us about twenty minutes to pull onto a large property full of tall trees that block out the sky. When we pull up to an elaborate gate designed into a beautiful tree with roots, the driver rolls down his window to enter a code into the security system. The gate opens, splitting the tree in half as it does, and we drive through. It's then that I see the house...or rather, mansion. "I didn't think we had anything like this in Oregon," I say.

"No one knows it's here, and we like to keep it that way. This is our home when we are in the mortal realm for business. It will be your home when you come here, under guard of course, for your monthly visits. You are never to bring anyone here. No one must know about it."

"You guys must be the life of the party," I mutter.

He ignores me as we pull up to the front door.

"Will I be meeting all of you now?" I'm nervous at the prospect of being in the same room with seven demonic vampires, one of whom I'm supposed to choose as a mate. I think that's a reasonable fear, at this point.

"No, the rest are busy at the moment. I'll take you to our world and bring you to High Castle."

A castle? "What's it like? Hell?"

"You'll see soon enough."

I'm still clutching my bag tightly when we enter the mansion and he gives me a ridiculously fast tour. I try to keep track of it all in my head. Tall ceilings, beautifully polished furniture, tapestries and paintings hanging from the walls, a huge stone fireplace in the living quarters with deep couches and chairs in red and gold fabric. Wall sized television in another room with surround-sound speakers. The kitchen is a dream, stocked with everything a gourmet cook would need to make a masterpiece. "Do vampires eat?"

"We do," he says. "The living on blood alone is a myth. We need blood, but we need food too."

At least, once I'm turned, I won't have to give up food. That's good news.

"What about the sun?"

"We cannot be in the human sun. It burns us. But our world has its own sun that does us no harm."

"Why?"

"Why what?"

"Why any of it? The blood. The sun. Why would our world be so inhospitable to you at the same time as it is so necessary for your survival."

"Curses aren't meant to be pleasant," he says, snickering.

"Who cursed you?"

"Our uncle, of course. Really, it's like you know nothing." I try to argue, but he continues. "Come on now. We have to hurry." He walks me through the halls and shows me door after door, explaining which prince they belong to. He stops in front of the last door in the hall. "This is your room."

I open it and see a four-poster canopy bed with cream and gold bedding. A fire roars opposite the window, and a small couch, chair and table are set to one side. An armoire and dresser with a vanity are set on the other.

"You have your own private washroom," he says, pointing to a door by the dresser. "I'll leave you to freshen up and then we venture forth. I've taken the liberty of providing suitable clothing for you. Please use them."

I look down at my jeans and t-shirt. "What's wrong with what I'm wearing?"

"You are being presented to our people as the future Princess, and Queen. You cannot arrive looking as you do."

When he leaves, I drop my bag on the floor and look through the dresser and armoire. It is filled with silks and satins and shoes I'm not sure I could walk in. There's a knock at the door, and before I can answer an older woman enters. She's dressed in a long black dress that is entirely functional. Her hair is greying and pulled into a tight bun. "My name is Mrs. Landon, and I've been sent to help you dress," she says in a British accent.

"I'm quite sure I can dress on my own, but thank you."

"Nonsense," she says. "I'm here to help." She opens the armoire and pulls out a sleeveless white satin gown. "This goes well with your complexion. Now off with your clothes."

While I undress self-consciously, she hands me lace panties and shoes that match the dress. Once I've put on my undergarments, she has me step into the dress, then she buttons up the row of satin buttons on my back. There are no zippers, and I wonder how I'll ever get this off. Once she is done, she pulls my hair into a French twist and then directs me to sit in front of the vanity while she does my makeup. I barely recognize myself when she's done.

She hands me a long coat of soft white fur—faux I hope—and nods her head. "That will do well. Be off with you now. The Prince is waiting."

"Where am I to go?" I barely remember the layout of this place.

"Down the stairs. Just keep going down. You'll find a door at the bottom. Knock and he'll let you in."

I reach for my bag but she shakes her head. "You're not to bring anything with you. Just what you're wearing."

"Fine, but I want my necklace." I put the pendant on before she can protest, then pull the coat around my shoulders and leave the room. I find the winding stair case and follow it down. It stops at different levels in the mansion, but I keep walking until I find myself standing in front of an elaborate door carved from a very rich wood. I knock and wait. Asher opens. He's dressed formally, in a tuxedo of sorts, but not a modern one. It looks custom made and like something royalty would wear before clothing was mass produced.

He raises an eyebrow when he sees me. "You clean up quite well."

"I wasn't dirty," I say, stepping into the room with him.

It's nothing grand. A small room—relatively speaking—with stone walls, bookshelves lining them, a lone desk with a chair in the corner, and a mirror.

The mirror is the most remarkable piece. It's tall and smooth, made from a golden wood carved into beautiful images around the glass. Mermaids and dragons and fairies and all manner of fairytale scenes play out in the designs. I run a hand over the rich wood and shiver.

"That is our door to your new home," he says.

"Like a portal?"

"Exactly."

I can see myself in the mirror, my red lips and white dress, pale skin and black hair pulled up. Asher stands next to me, but he is invisible in the mirror. "So it's true? Vampires don't have reflections?"

"We can," he says. "Just not in mirrors. We'll show up in film and water reflections. But mirrors, all mirrors, are doorways to us, and thus do not allow reflections, but rather glimpses into another realm."

"So we could have gotten to your world through any mirror? Even one at my house?"

"We could get there using a pocket mirror if we so choose, though that manner of travel is a bit...pinched."

"Then why all this?" I ask, waving my hand at the extravagant mirror before us.

He shrugs. "What can I say? We have a flare for the dramatic. Are you ready?"

"If I'm not, would that change anything?"

"No. Not a thing. I was just trying to be polite."

"It doesn't suit you," I say.

"I'll keep that in mind."

"Why can't I bring my own stuff?" I ask. I'm mostly missing my phone. My one life-line back to my friends and my mother.

"You will see soon enough. Modern technology does not work in our world. We cannot bring anything with us that was made with machines or advancements our world doesn't have."

I frown at that. "Why?"

"It's part of our curse."

He offers me his arm, and I take it, trying not to let my hand shake too much.

And then he pulls me into the mirror.

I close my eyes, half expecting to crash into glass, but instead I sink into thick liquid. It doesn't feel wet, and I can still breathe.

My head spins, and lights and shadows play against my eye lids. I'm scared to open my eyes, to see what I've committed my soul to.

"You can look now, Princess," Asher says. "You're home. Welcome to hell."

5

PRINCE OF WAR

"Beware the princes of hell."
—the Warden

I open my eyes and suck in my breath. I was expecting fire and brimstone. Pain and suffering. Endless torture. What I see is something out of a fairytale. We stand on the bank of a lake, having just stepped through a large, ornate mirror that matches the one in the mansion back home. It's night, and a full moon is out. Another moon, a crescent one, hovers by its side. The stars are bright and big in the dark sky, much larger than the ones in my world. Before us, water stretches out into the distance, shimmering in the moonlight, and beneath the dark surface something glows a pale blue.

"Those are moon fish," Asher says, noticing my stare.

I look around and see more of them. I want to dip my hand in to splash at them, but for all I know they are carnivorous and would eat me as much as play with me. It's a peaceful moment, but I haven't forgotten where I am and why.

"We don't call this place hell," Asher says. "Here, it is known as the Isle of Inferna." He turns back to the mirror we just came from and places a hand on it. When he pulls his hand away, the reflection of the mirror shifts, the glass swirling in colors until a new image appears. At first, I can't tell what I'm looking at.

"This is Inferna," Asher says, pointing to what I can now see is a map. It looks like a floating island with seven concentric rings in the middle. I touch the center, which all the rings seem to protect, and the map zooms in, showing me a three dimensional close up of a grand castle.

"That's High Castle," Asher says. "I will be taking you there directly."

I shift my finger to see a wider view again. "What are these circles?"

"Those are the seven realms, each ruled by one of the princes. There are other maps of our kingdom but it's best seen from an enchanted mirror. For safety reasons, however, there are no mirrors allowed within the realms. Anyone wishing to travel by the gateways must come here, to the edge of the outer region, and then use the canals to get where they wish to go."

That's when I see a boat float up to the shore and stop for us. "Aren't we a bit overdressed for travel by boat?"

There is snow on the ground, and my heel sinks into it as I follow Asher towards the boat. I would have stayed in my jeans if I'd known we'd be traveling this way.

He side-eyes me. "Your dress will be fine."

I sigh as Asher climbs in first. Colorful pillows are artfully arranged on the wooden seats, and the prince sinks into them, watching with amusement as I navigate my way onto the precarious floating wood. It sways and I stand still, one foot on land, one in the boat.

Asher chuckles. "It's charmed to always stay upright. You can't tip it if you tried." To prove his point—or terrify me—I'm honestly not sure which, he grabs the sides and shakes the boat.

It moves, but only a little. He grins. "See? You're safe."

Emboldened despite his attitude, I climb in and recline against my own pillows. They are surprisingly comfortable.

Asher says something under his breath once I'm settled and the boat begins to glide through the water. "I've never been on a boat before, but I'm pretty sure it usually involves motors or rowing."

"Your world may have the marvels of electronics, but we have magic. In a toss between the two, I'd always choose the latter."

My eyes widen. "Magic? Real magic?" For some reason, this is harder to grasp than demons and vampires, though I'm not sure why. Particularly since I just traveled to another world through an enchanted mirror.

"Real magic. Wielded carefully, of course. In the wrong hands, magic is dangerous. There are laws about the proper use of magic, for everyone's protection."

"So you can wield magic?"

"Not exactly. I—really anyone—can use a spell once it's been cast. But vampires and demons cannot cast magic."

"Then who casts the spells?"

"The Fae," he says, then falls silent.

I have so many more questions, but he doesn't seem to be of a mood to talk anymore, so I entertain myself by getting to know my new world. The lake we've been floating on has begun to narrow, taking us into a canal with forests on either side of us. We pass between two giant walls that span as far as I can see. At least six stories high, they seem carved from one mass of gray stone. Above us, connecting the two walls, hangs a metal gate forged from interlocking beams.

Asher notices me looking. "So we can close the canals during an attack."

"From who?" I ask.

"Enemies my people have made. They live in limbo, the Outlands, beyond these walls."

I raise an eyebrow. "And how often are you attacked?"

"There are occasional raids. But first, they must deal with the archers on the walls. If they make it past, then we have soldiers on the ground." He speaks casually, as if this is the day to day of his life. Will I too, one day, speak of raids and battle so easily?

We pass the walls, and the temperature drops, and I pull my coat around me, shivering at such a sudden change in climate.

"We've entered my brother's realm, the Prince of War," he says. "It's miserably cold here this time of year."

Majestic mountains topped with caps of snow reach into the sky, and trees so tall I can't see their tops line the shore. In the distance, a castle forged from stone is carved into the side of a massive peak. Red flags fly from two towers, depicting a white wolf. "Do other people live here?" I wonder out loud.

"Yes. Each realm has its villages, its center, and its populace. Most are demons but there are other kinds here as well. It's important you always stay within the realms. We aren't the only race inhabiting this land, and believe it or not, we're the good guys. You don't want to go beyond the gates, if you value your life. Or your mother's."

Asher's voice drops to a low rumble, and I shiver at the weight in his words. What kinds of creatures live outside the realms that would have vampires scared of them? I can't even imagine. "Speaking of my mother, when will I get to see her?"

"We will head there first, to set your mind at ease. Then you will be assigned a realm to begin your stay with us. My brothers were meant to decide the order while I retrieved you."

"The order?"

Asher looks over at me and smirks. "Yes, the order. You must spend time with each of us before you make your choice. You'll have a month with each prince. At the end of the seven months, you will decide who amongst us will be your mate and future king."

"So my mother has to live as a prisoner for seven months? What if I decide sooner?"

His smirk disappears and he leans closer to me, his cologne making my head spin. "Be very careful, princess. My brothers are ruthless demons who have lived more lifetimes than you can imagine. They have their own agendas and will do whatever it takes to accomplish them. Do not be hasty in this. Not only are you sealing your own fate for all eternity, but our kingdom's as well."

"Why?"

He blinks. "Why what?"

"Why leave such an important decision to an ordinary human? Why not just fight it out or use magic or something to decide the next king?"

He leans back and crosses his hands over his lap. "Why indeed. For starters, you are far less ordinary than you imagine yourself to be. And then of course you know the rest of the answer." He chuckles. "You are the chosen one, there is a prophecy, and danger, and, of course, my sexy charms. Isn't that what you said in the hospital? You weren't wrong, princess. You weren't all the way right, but you weren't wrong."

I glare at him. "Thanks. That clears everything right up."

Our boat turns, and the landscape changes once again. It's still cold, but not nearly the frigid weather of before. We are no longer surrounded by the ruggedly wild forests. Instead, we travel through a city full of tall buildings that look grown from stone and trees. A white marble tower blocks out one of the moons, green vines spiraling up from its base. Immaculate gardens adorn almost every dwelling, full of silver and purple flowers, their sweet aromas fresh on the wind. Everything looks smooth and polished: elegant symbols carved into the walls, delicate archways crossing over cobbled streets. This time I do see an occasional person walking around, alone or with one or two others. It's late, but the city is lit with light from glowing blue orbs that seems to hover in the air. "What is this place?" I ask.

The prince smiles, and for the first time it seems to be with genuine pleasure. "This is my realm. Beautiful, isn't it?"

"Very," I say honestly.

"It is my pride," he says, then laughs. "After all, I am the Prince of Pride."

I can't help but laugh with him at his own stupid humor, and for a moment we share in a very normal camaraderie of two people enjoying something lovely together.

"My location is less than optimal," he says, "placed between the wild lands of War and the dreariness of Envy. Honestly, he really needs to do something with his life. His land could be beautiful, in its own way. It's heavy with red clay that bleeds like blood into the snow in winter, and he gets the most dreadful storms, but the rock formations that litter his coast lines are actually quite dramatic and stunning, if paired with the right architecture. Unfortunately, he has no eye for design and thus his realm languishes under his artless care." His voice is full of dramatic despondency, like a petulant child who didn't get his choice of toy for the holiday. "You'll see what I mean soon enough. We're almost there."

The canal twists to the right and our boat magically follows. As we turn, the trees become more dispersed, and instead the water is framed by pillars of rock and stone, slate grey and weathered by time and the elements. Our boat lurches and comes to a sudden stop, sending me spiraling forward into Asher, who catches me in his arms.

"No need to throw yourself at me just yet," he says with a smirk. "We'll have our time together soon enough."

I roll my eyes and shove away from him. "Cute." We still aren't moving, but I can't see what caused us to stop. "Did the magic fail?" I ask.

He shakes his head. "Not possible." His face loses its chronic arrogance and falls into a look of real concern as his eyes scan the canal. He dips his hand into the water, deep enough that his sleeve becomes wet. "There's a felled tree at the bottom blocking the boat," he says, pulling his hand out. "We need to move it before we can continue."

"I assume this is where magic comes in handy?"

He chuckles humorously. "It would be, if either of us could wield it. Unfortunately, we'll have to do things the old fashioned way."

"Bet you're glad we dressed for this party now, aren't you?" I wink at him as the boat glides to the banks.

He stands and steps out carefully, then offers his hand. "Cloth can be cleaned. It is not of consequence."

"Right." I can tell he hates this, and that somehow makes my discomfort more bearable. I'd give anything to be in jeans right now. My white dress remains mostly unscathed as I climb out of the boat and stand in front of a giant slab of grey stone, but my shoes don't fare as well sinking into the muck on the edge of the canal. I give up and take them off, tossing them back into the boat so I can walk barefoot.

Asher looks ready to argue, but I hold up a hand. "You want to trade shoes? No? Then shove it."

He makes the smart choice, and his mouth snaps closed. He leans over to pull the boat out of the water and over the fallen tree. I'm about to offer to help lift, but...

He doesn't need my help. Somehow, Asher manages to lift the whole boat by himself. His muscles bulge under his clothes, but his face shows no sign of the effort it must take to lift something that heavy.

He's placing it back in the water on the other side of the tree, when I hear a branch snap.

I start to spin, but I'm too slow.

Someone grabs me from behind, covering my mouth with a cloth so I can't scream. I bite instead, and the hand loosens, but only for a moment. The arms around me tighten, and though I try my hardest, I can't push them away. I struggle anyways, unwilling to make myself an easier target than I already am.

There's something on the cloth over my mouth, a chemical smell, and it makes me light headed.

Someone is trying to kidnap me. Someone followed me here.

My eyes go wide with panic, even as I begin to lose control of my limbs, going limp in my assailant's grip.

Blurry images enter my view, more attackers, at least ten. They draw swords.

Asher turns around and screams, a primal sound not of fear but rage. He charges forward, lightning fast. I can barely see him as he darts around, disarming one opponent and taking their blade. Steel clashes. Mud splatters. Blood sprays over my face.

My captor drags me back, away from the fighting, between towers of stone. He wears brown furs and a leather hood, shrouding his face. I can't make out more; my eyes grow heavy.

My attacker stumbles.

I focus all my remaining strength.

And ram the back of my head into his face.

Pain explodes in my skull, and I hear the crunch of bones. Probably his nose. He curses, letting go, and I fall, slamming into gravel. I scream at the top of my lungs, hoping someone in this realm will care and come to help. I can't walk, so I crawl, my knees scraping against rock, my hands bleeding from tiny cuts.

In the distance, three men surround Asher, but he holds his own, fighting with such speed and agility my eyes can't follow. But they are fast too, and I wonder if vampires can be killed.

The drug they used on me dulls all my senses, and I collapse near the water.

Then I hear it.

The sound of hooves.

Of wolves howling.

Of warriors shouting.

Asher's voice is sharp with relief, but still filled with his normal snark. "Good of you to finally join us, brother."

Swords clash. Blood seeps into the earth.

Visions mix around me. It's hard to breathe. Hard to think.

Then all goes quiet.

And a wet nose nudges my face. I pry my eyes open and see the face of a large white wolf staring at me, his golden eyes too intelligent for comfort.

"He normally hates anyone but me." The voice is familiar. Comforting. Deep and gravelly.

Arms scoop me from the ground and as my head falls back, I see the face I knew would be there. "Fenris?"

Fen looks down at me. "You really should stop getting drugged and nearly kidnapped."

I muster some indignation, though I can tell I won't be conscious much longer. "People really should stop drugging and nearly kidnapping me," I mumble.

It's his laugh I hear as darkness takes me.

...

I wake in silk sheets that feel too soft, too slippery to be entirely comfortable. The bed is large and plush and I am dressed in...something I don't recognize. My head doesn't hurt nearly as badly this time around when I open my eyes.

The room flickers with the light of a fire dancing off the walls. I push myself up in bed to look around.

"Drink this." A pewter goblet is handed to me.

I look over and see Fen sitting in a chair by my bed, a massive white wolf sleeping by his feet. Or at least pretending to sleep. I have a sense that wolf is acutely aware of everything happening in this room and beyond. "You!" I push the goblet away and glare at Fen. "You're one of them and you lied to me."

"I never lied to you. I just didn't tell you everything. For that matter, you didn't share all your secrets that day either, did you?" His blue eyes catch the light of the fire and seem to spark. He's dressed differently then last time I saw him. Brown leather pants and shirt, heavy fur boots.

"Well, no. But that's different. I didn't know you knew about this stuff. You knew I did."

"Fair enough," he says, still holding the goblet out to me. "But my job was to keep you safe. It was Asher's job to get you here of your own free will. I couldn't interfere. Now drink this before your headache hits."

I take the cup from him and sniff, then wrinkle my nose. "This is awful. What's in it?"

"You don't want to know, but you do want to drink it. It's the reason you don't feel like you've been drugged, but the dose you had earlier has nearly worn off."

I remember how long it took me to recover last time, and I plug my nose and gulp the vile liquid down, nearly gagging as I do. It doesn't taste as bad as it smells. It tastes worse.

I throw the goblet at Fen when I'm done, but he catches it one-handed with a chuckle. "Feeling feisty, I see."

"Still angry you lied to me. I trusted you."

He stands, shaking his head. "You shouldn't trust anyone here, Princess. Let that be your first lesson." He walks to the door, his wolf following him.

"Not even you?" I ask.

"Especially not me," he says, opening the door. "Now get dressed. Asher is waiting for you in the library. I'm to take you there and make sure no one else tries to kill you in the meantime."

"And who is trying to kill me?"

He pauses. "The Fae who dwell in the Outlands."

Fae? Are they the dangerous enemy Asher spoke of? The magic wielders. "And why are they after me?"

"I suspect it is because they know of your importance. If you were to be taken, then we would have no king, and our kingdom would remain disorganized. Now, hurry and change."

I look down at the silver nightgown someone dressed me in. "Where are my clothes? How did I end up in this?"

"You were covered in blood and mud. I thought you'd be more comfortable this way. There are clothes in the wardrobe that should fit you. This will be your room when you're at High Castle."

My face burns. "*You* changed me?" I'm trying to imagine how that went while I was unconscious, but my mind keeps freezing every time I imagine his hands on my body. Naked.

"Relax. I didn't touch anything I shouldn't. Your virtue is intact."

I snort. "I'm not worried about my virtue. What century do you think this is? I'm worried about consent."

He raises an eyebrow, then crosses the room in two long strides until he's leaning over me. "I assure you, Princess, if we ever consummate anything between us, it will be entirely mutual."

His presence, the sheer headiness of his scent, of his body so close to mine, makes me dizzy, but I pull myself together fast enough to respond before he walks away. "As it should be."

There's a pause between us that seems to linger beyond the confines of time, where only he and I exist. I have to fight the urge to lift my hand and run it against his jaw, to feel the stubble of his five o'clock shadow. To pull him closer to me.

His eyes are locked on mine, but then his wolf growls at the door and our moment is broken. Before I can blink Fen turns to the door and Asher approaches.

"Settle him down, Fen. It's just me." Asher enters the room and stands by the fire, leaving plenty of space between him and the wolf. "I see our girl is awake. Excellent. There are places to see, people to meet, things to do."

"I want to see my mother," I say, pulling myself out of bed. My legs are wobbly, but otherwise I feel fine. That medicine really does work well.

Asher frowns. "About that…"

"No. I'm not doing anything else until I confirm she is here and safe." I lock eyes with him, my arms crossed over my chest. I'm not backing down on this one.

Fen leans against the wall, grinning at Asher.

The Prince of Pride frowns back. "You think this is amusing, brother? Wait until it's your turn to deal with her."

Fen snickers. "I'm the one who keeps rescuing her, while she's supposed to be under your care." His wolf bares his teeth at Asher.

"All right, enough bickering," I say. "Both of you out. I need to change." I shoo them through the door and close it behind them, then take a deep breath. It's time to see what I've gotten myself into.

...

When I exit my room, both Asher and Fen are still there, looking mildly uncomfortable with each other. Asher frowns when he sees what I'm wearing, but Fen's lip twitches, and I can tell he's pleased.

"This is not an outfit suited for a princess!" says Asher. I swear he's about to wring his hands in distress, and I almost giggle.

There were dresses galore in the wardrobe, but in one of the drawers tucked into the back, I found some-thing better. Black leather pants, boots, and a red cor-set with a black cloak. I feel pretty badass, to be honest. And though it's not the most comfortable outfit I've ever worn, I'm happy in it. My hair is tied into braids, and I put on red lipstick to match my corset. I just need a sword and I'll be set. Swords seem big here. Fen car-ries one at his hip. Yes, I definitely need my own sword. And I'll need to learn how to use it.

"I think she looks like the perfect princess," Fen says.

I try not to smile at his compliment. I'm still angry at him for lying to me, but there's so much going on I don't understand. I'm not sure how to feel about anyone right now.

Asher just shakes his head at us and begins walking down the hall. I follow and Fen walks just behind me, presumably acting as guard. I should feel more nervous with him and that wolf trailing after me, but I don't. It's actually reassuring knowing he's there. I don't get to see much of the castle, mostly hallways, covered in murals depicting battles and harvests. Above an extravagant door hangs a giant painting of an older man, his hair black and streaked with grey, his face pale and smooth. He wears a black vest and cape, his buttons gold.

"Who's that?" I ask.

Fen doesn't look at the painting, scowling for some reason.

Asher sighs. "Our father, King Lucian. He could be...difficult, at times, but he was always fair."

Fen chuckles, though there is no humor to it. "Fair to you, perhaps."

"Now, now brother. This is no time for bickering."

"Time for truth perhaps."

Asher shakes his head, turning to me. "Excuse my brother. Our father's loss has affected us all in different ways." He faces Fen. "Let us take the princess to her mother. We can discuss this later."

Fen nods, though I wish he hadn't. I want to know more about what happened to the king.

Asher takes a right down a hall and pulls a thick iron key from his pocket. He opens a dusty black door, revealing a staircase winding down. The path is lit by torches that flicker a blue light, but still I trip, knocking into Asher, who catches me and steadies me before continuing. I hear Fen's wolf growl when Asher touches me, and Asher scowls at the beast.

We descend deeper until we reach another door. Asher opens it, and we walk into a dark hall, full of stone and metal bars.

"I shall wait here and guard the entrance," Fen says, stopping by the door.

Asher frowns. "Of course."

The wolf sits by Fen's feet, ears alert, teeth bared at the dungeon.

It's hot, the stone walls are stained red, and I don't even want to think of what caused those marks. I cough. "Is that sulfur?"

"Yes," he says.

"How disappointingly predictable. A demon dungeon that smells of sulfur."

"It has its uses," he says, but I can tell he's bothered by being called disappointing and predictable. He is the Prince of Pride after all.

There is a sound of clanking chains as we approach a corner, and the largest man I've ever seen appears before us. He's not really a man though. He's at least nine feet tall, bulging with muscle everywhere. His head is bald and his body covered in tribal tattoos. Large black horns protrude from his skull. His pupils are too narrow, like a reptile's. His teeth are sharpened to deadly points and when he speaks, his voice sounds like gravel. "My Prince, how can I serve you?"

He doesn't look at me at all, but I can tell he's aware of my presence. I know he sees everything I might do before I even do it. This man-beast terrifies me.

"Please allow Miss Spero to see her mother's soul, and then we will be going."

The demon pauses, uncertainty on his face. "If you feel that is wise, Your Highness?"

"Just do it. I'm in a bit of a hurry and must be on with it."

"Of course."

He leads us through more halls stained with the remnants of their last occupants and opens a barred door, the metal hinges creaking loudly in the eerie silence. The room is large, like an underground warehouse, and full of giant cages hanging from the ceiling yet low to the ground. Each has the glowing ethereal form of a human laying on it. There must be hundreds of them, at least. Maybe more.

"She is here," he says, walking to a cage in the middle.

I shuffle forward, my body shaking. I see my mother's soul, leaning against the cold bars. It is transparent, ghostly, but it is her. She looks the same as her body, and I reach to touch her, but my hand finds no purchase.

"She is not here in form," Asher says. "Only in spirit."

"Can I speak with her?" I ask.

He shakes his head. "If she is awoken, she will suffer greatly. My father recently ordered that all souls be kept asleep during their time with us. It used to be standard practice that they remain awake, tortured and in misery. Some demons feed off that pain."

"That's barbaric." My voice trembles just imaging my mother, or anyone, enduring such a nightmarish existence.

"That is likely why the King ended it," Asher says, and I can hear in his voice a softening when he speaks of his father. "He had a change of heart near the end. I still…Never mind."

"What?"

His eyes are dark and heavy. "I still wonder why. Why did an eternal demon change his ways?" He looks at me, his gaze piercing. "What changed his heart?"

We are both silent for a moment, and I turn away, the intensity of his glance overwhelming.

"He should have kept things as they were," says the demon warden.

Asher's eyes widen, and he turns to the warden, grabbing him by the neck. He squeezes, choking the giant, bringing him to his knees. Asher's fangs descend. "You dare speak of your King, of the royal family, that way?"

I watch, amazed. Asher is impressive in his own right, but nothing in bulk compared to the dungeon-beast, and yet, the demon seems terrified of the Prince.

"Apologies, Master. It will not happen again."

"See that it doesn't, or you will suffer a much worse fate than those sorry souls once did."

I turn my attention back to my mother and watch her for a few more moments before Asher puts a hand on my shoulder. "You've seen her. I have fulfilled my promise. We must be going now."

He turns to walk out and I follow him, but as I reach the end of the room, the demon grabs my elbow. I pull away, instant panic filling my veins. His eyeteeth elongate and his pupils dilate, but he doesn't try to bite me. Instead, he leans down to whisper into my ear. "Beware the princes of hell. Not all of them are pleased that you will decide on the next king. Not all of them wish you alive."

6

THE SEVEN REALMS
OF HELL

"Don't let the pretty baubles fool you, Princess. We are
still demons. This is still a dangerous place."

—Fenris Vane

I rush out the door and into the arms of Fen.

The air immediately cools, and I suck in a breath and
sag against Fen's chest. He stiffens in surprise and I realize what I'm doing and pull back. "Er…sorry about that.
The, uh, guard in there scared me and…" My voice trails
and I really have no idea what to say next so I take another
step back, but end up bumping into the stone wall behind
me. Fenris is still staring at me, his blue eyes pulling me
into him as he steps closer. His wolf is by his side and
scoots forward with his master, his eyes on us both.

Fen is so close to me now I can smell the wildness
that clings to him like a cologne. He inhales deeply, his

eyes unreadable, and his eyeteeth elongate. His eyes drop to my neck, and I know I should be scared. A vampire is checking me out like I'm dinner. But I'm not scared. I'm...entranced. A low growl vibrates in his throat as he leans in. "You should be more careful, Princess."

His breath brushes against my neck, sending a chill down my spine. "My name isn't Princess, or girl, it's Ari. Arianna if you want to be formal."

Fen looks at me with a strange expression, like he's trying to figure out what I am.

"Time to go," says Asher from the top of the stairs, once again interrupting something that feels heavy. The wolf, whose name I really must learn soon, reverts into his defensive position.

"Does your wolf basically hate everyone but you?" I ask.

Fen looks down at him. "Usually, yes. You seem to be the exception."

Asher clears his throat. "Sorry to interrupt you two, but Dean is waiting and you know how patient he is."

Fen pulls away from me and turns to face Asher. "Dean can wait as long as needed. I care little for whatever so-called demands he has on his time."

"Be that as it may, we still must go. Unless you two are planning to stay in the dungeon all night?"

I shiver at the thought, and the wolf steps away from Fen to come closer to me, pushing his large head against my leg until I pet him. Both the princes stare at us, open jawed, for several seconds.

Asher is the first to break the silence. "What the—?"

Fen crosses his arms over his chest. "He's been like that since she got here. I've never seen anything like it."

"The other brothers are not going to like this, Fenris. They will feel you are taking liberties to weigh things in your favor."

Watching the two of them is like watching the North and South Pole in an odd dance. They are so different—Asher with his fine suits and refinement and Fen with his wildness and leather—but somehow they compliment each other in a strange way.

Fen scoffs at Asher's words. "I care as much about that bloody throne as I do about Dean's latest conquest, which is to say not at all. They should know that. This isn't my game, it's all of yours."

"Be that as it may, this will ruffle feathers."

Fen pulls his eyes from me and the wolf to turn to Asher. "I'll do more than ruffle feathers if any of them dare challenge me."

The warden's warning echoes in my mind. Is Fen one of those displeased at my presence?

Asher holds up his hands in surrender. "I'm on your side in this, brother. You know that."

Fen nods his head once sharply, and begins walking up the staircase back to the main castle. His wolf stays by my side until Fen turns, face puckered with irritation. He whistles, and the wolf rubs against me again, whining. "Oh for the love of all that's unholy, what is wrong with you, Baron?"

I'm starting to feel bad for Fen, so I nudge Baron with my hand. "Go on. I'll be okay."

He looks up at me, his eyes so intelligent, and almost nods, then slowly moves to Fen, but keeps looking back to make sure I'm coming. I stifle a grin and hurry up the stairs as Fen curses and turns away from us. Asher watches with a mix of amusement and worry on his face.

As we make our way to wherever Asher is taking us, I ask the question I've been wanting an answer to for some time. "Are we going to talk about the fact that these Fae keep attacking me?"

"No," Fen says gruffly. I think he's still mad about his wolf not obeying him.

"If they do manage to kidnap me, what are they planning to do?"

"Shut you up, hopefully."

Yup, he's still mad.

"Look, I'm sorry your wolf likes someone else for the first time ever, but that's no reason to act like a petulant child. There are serious matters to discuss here."

Asher laughs out loud. "She's got your number, brother!"

Fen turns and grabs him by his collar, shoving him against the stone wall. "That is quite enough from you, *brother*. I've done everything you've asked. I kept her safe. I got her here. I'm done." He releases Asher—who doesn't look the least bit scared—and storms away, leaving us alone in the passageway. His wolf does follow this time, though reluctantly when he sees I'm not joining him.

Asher adjusts his clothing and brushes away the wrinkles caused by his brother's rough handling. "Fen has a bit of a temper," Asher says calmly. "Prince of War and all. You understand."

"I understand that a family of immortal vampires has all of eternity and still can't figure out how to grow up," I say. I'm tired of the bickering, so I walk ahead, but once we come to the door that brought us here, I pause, unsure of where we're going.

Asher grins, winking at me, and leads me through hallways lined with gilded doors and gold trimmed paintings and elaborate doorways carved out of stone or marble or wood into beautiful shapes. We stop in a hall with a fire blazing in the largest stone fireplace I've ever seen. There are pillows and rugs in front of the fire for lounging, with tables filled with drink and food, and plush, elegant furniture artfully placed throughout the room to create reading and conversation nooks. One wall is lined with books and another is a painted mural of a beautiful landscape with a Pegasus flying through a winter storm. In the center of the room stands one of the most beautiful men I've ever seen.

He has the kind of physical beauty that is literally stunning. Golden hair that falls around his shoulders in thick waves. Eyes so piercing blue they hurt to look at. Skin carved of golden marble. A face that could slay armies with its beauty. A body that is so perfect he looks unreal. Like, I can't walk anymore, because I'm *literally* stunned into place.

When he sees me, he smiles and I nearly choke on my own tongue.

Asher sees my response and just sighs. "Arianna, this is Dean. Dean, this is the princess."

Dean reaches for my hand and brings it to his lips. The kiss is soft, tender, and stays on my skin like a gift. "Hello, Princess Arianna. It is a pleasure to finally meet you. I look forward to our time together and trust you will enjoy yourself *in all ways*."

Parts of my body I've neglected most of my life are set on fire by his words, and I have no response but to stand there, weak-kneed and shaking.

Dean is still holding my hand, and I don't pull away until Asher nudges me. "Arianna, the council has chosen Dean, Prince of Lust, to be your first guide in our world. You will spend a month with him, and then move to the next realm with another prince."

I blink, reminding myself who I am and why I'm here. "Of course. It's nice to meet you Dean." I take a deep breath to steady myself and finally pull my hand away. It still burns with his lips, and I find it very disconcerting. It's not as if Fen and Asher are slouches. They are prime male specimens in their own right. But I can see why Dean got the title Prince of Lust.

A growl diverts Dean's attention from me, as Baron approaches us. He nudges against my side and my hand falls on his head. His presence clears my mind, saving me from whatever fog of desire Dean casts by mere proximity.

"Actually, that is incorrect," Fenris says, joining us. "The council chose me as her first escort, so she'll be coming to my realm."

Dean scowls at Fenris. "You relinquished your rights to being first. I believe your exact words were, 'I'll not be a pawn in this game you are all playing, so sod off and have at her.'"

"Have at her?" I ask, fire burning in my stomach. "I'm not a thing to be had at by any of you! Not by charm," I say, looking at Asher, "or brute force," that was for Fen, "or by a pretty face." I glare at Dean who looks as shocked as Fen did when his wolf snuggled up to me. "You lot have got to stop acting like asses and start behaving like reasonably intelligent men, or I have no idea how I'll fulfill my contract of picking any of you!"

"Well, brother," Asher says to Fen through a smirk, "looks like you have an interesting month ahead of you."

"Wait a second now, I haven't agreed to relinquish my turn," Dean says.

Asher shrugs. "You don't have to. Fen is right. The council chose him and he has the right to reclaim her."

Dean turns to Fen, his face in a scowl. "You're an ass, you know that? There's a reason no one likes you."

Asher laughs as Dean storms out of the room, but Fen's face is all serious. I think his brother's words bothered him. Or maybe he's regretting his 'claim' to me already.

When Dean is out of earshot, Asher calms himself and turns to Fen. "What's going on? This isn't like you."

"It's my job to keep her safe," Fen says.

"And you've done an admirable job," Asher says. "But despite Dean's arrogance and frivolous life, he's as capable as any at fighting. No harm will come to her in his realm."

Fen sighs. "Have you not pieced it together yet? How did the Fae get all the way to Envy's realm to attempt another kidnapping? For that matter, how did the Fae reach the High Castle to assassinate our father? Have you not wondered?"

Asher frowns. "Of course I have but—" his eyes widen. "You're not suggesting what I think you are?"

Fen nods. "The *only* way is if one of us let them in."

"Fenris, this is a serious accusation. You're suggesting that one of our brothers not only plots to kidnap Arianna, but also helped aid in our father's murder?"

"I'm not suggesting it," Fen says. "I'm saying that's exactly what happened."

"If you're right, then why share your suspicions with me? How do you know I'm not the guilty party?" Asher asks. "For that matter, how do I know it's not you?"

"You know it's not me because I don't want to be High King. And I'm pretty sure it's not you because I trust you more than most. That and you had plenty of time with Arianna in her world and never made a move. You could have made it much easier to kidnap her, but you didn't. So it must be one of the others."

The princes lock eyes with each other. I might as well not be here but for Baron standing by my side. The ramifications of what they are saying slowly sinks into my mind. I have to spend a month with each brother. If one of them is a traitor, then like it or not, I will eventually be kidnapped. And I still don't know why the princes wanted me here to begin with.

"I get why the Fae are after me. Basically you put a target on my head when you decided I, and only I, could decide the fate of this kingdom. But you still haven't explained why you chose me. Why am *I* so important to *you*?"

Asher frowns. "To answer that would require bringing our father back from the dead. He dictated the terms of the ascension in his will. He is the one who negotiated the contract for your mother's soul. And he is the one who demanded you be brought here to marry one of us before a new reign could occur. We don't know why, and it has caused a considerable amount of unrest amongst our brothers, who are not happy their fate—and this kingdom's fate—rests in the hands of a human girl."

"Which is why," Fen says, "we must leave this place. I need to get you to my realm, where you will be safe while we sort this out and figure out who has betrayed us."

Fenris nods to Asher and turns to leave the room. Asher reaches for my hand. "Be safe, Arianna. I will see you again soon."

I follow Fen out, his wolf trailing by my side, and he takes me to the castle's entrance. A chandelier hangs overhead, made of crystal branches and glowing leaves casting shadows against the walls. The doors are tall, wide, made from thick wood and carved with a tree symbol. Fenris opens them and Baron nudges me through.

It's still dark, well past midnight, and the sky is bright with the moons and stars. Once again I'm taken to a boat. "Is this really the fastest mode of transportation you have?"

"Yes. Get in."

It's a lot easier in pants and boots than a dress and heels. The wolf leaps in next to me and lays his large head on my lap as the boat begins to magically move through the water. It's a warm night, which I wasn't expecting. I slip off my black cloak and lay it by my side. "The air smells different here," I say. "More...dry than your realm did."

Fen raises an eyebrow. "You have a tracker's nose. That could be useful. We are about to enter Niam's land. The Prince of Greed, as you might know him. It's a desert land that doesn't provide much in the way of export, but does manage all the commerce in our kingdom."

"So Niam is the tax collector? He must be popular."

Fen chuckles. "You could say that. He's also the banker. All things money, that's Niam."

We travel through his realm, and though it's dark, I can make out the city hub through the waves of sand. It's beautiful in its own way, with a cathedral in the center made of sandstone and a marketplace littered with colorful booths displaying wares. Right now they are closed up, but I can imagine the bustle of it all.

I have so many questions, but I'm exhausted and too tired to ask them right now. Fen is leaning against the pillows with his eyes closed, but I can tell he's as alert as ever. Does this man ever relax? I'm thinking no.

I mindlessly pet Baron, who snuggles in closer to me, his nose nudging my hand for more affection.

"There must be something special about you," Fen says.

"Because of your father's will?"

He opens his eyes to look at me. "No. Because of Baron. He's never taken to anyone but me before. I found him when he was a pup. Raiders from the Outlands had killed his litter, but he survived by some miracle, though he was nearly dead. Our healer said he was touched by a special magic, but that his condition was grave. I nursed him back to health, never leaving his side for nearly two weeks. If he likes you, which clearly he does, there must be something special about you."

"Is that why you intervened with Dean? Because your wolf likes me?"

"I told you why I did that."

"To protect me? I don't think that's the whole truth. Dean has quite the effect on women, doesn't he?"

Fen grunts. "Not just women. But yes. He does. It's part of his demon charms."

"And what are your demon charms?" I ask.

"Killing."

"Huh. That's less charming than you might imagine."

The landscape changes around us as the desert begins to transform into a more tropical, lush setting.

"Who lives here?" I ask. There's a sensual quality to this realm that permeates the sights, sounds, colors. From the boat we can see the city's center, and unlike Niam's realm, this place is still lively in the middle of the night. Women walk around in bathing suit tops of gold, silver and purple, with thin, sheer, colorful scarves of fabric draped around their lithe bodies. The men are dressed in less, bulging muscles oiled and glowing under the lights. Music plays, a deep rhythmic beat, and many dance, the movements nearly sexual as the bodies rub against each other. "Wait, let me guess? Lust?"

"Yes. And the source of most of the entertainment in our kingdom. Dean's is the most useless realm if you ask me."

The air is scented with oils and fragrant flowers, and I inhale deeply. "I don't know about that. There's something to be said for touch, love, laughter, entertainment. At least for humans, these things are important. They nourish us, feed our imagination, soothe our souls. Maybe your people aren't so different."

"These are all distractions, for humans or demons, it matters not."

He falls silent, arms crossed over his chest, but I still have questions. "How are such different climates supported so closely together?"

Fen shrugs. "It's the magic of this place. One could ask the same of your world, where you have snow topped mountains not far from beaches. Ours is just more compact."

I'm beginning to doze off, but the wolf nudges me as we enter a new realm.

Fen is sitting up now, more alert than before.

"Is everything okay?"

He nods. "Just being cautious. We're in Ace's realm now."

His realm is full of marvels. Though it's the middle of the night, there are people up and about tinkering with gadgets that look complicated and impressive. They work in shops under giant lamp posts, and the houses look busy too, with smoke drifting from chimneys and windows glowing with yellow light. It's like the whole realm is one big inventor's workshop. Wood, metal, stone...all of it is used in ways I couldn't have imagined. One device is turning water into steam to power another device that cuts wood. "What's his sin?"

"Sloth."

"Seriously? This looks the opposite of slothful."

"He is a bit of a contradiction. Ace is brilliant. He's also lazy, or so he says. I've never actually witnessed said laziness myself. But he claims if you want to know the easiest, fastest and best way to get something done, give it to a lazy person. Thus, he invents things to make life easier for everyone."

There's a loud explosion in the distance and a pillar of fire and smoke rise to the sky. "What was that?"

"A failed invention," Fen says with affection. "Any closer and we'd hear Ace swearing and cursing about now."

"This isn't what I was expecting hell to be like," I admit, leaning back against my pillows.

"It never is. But don't let the pretty baubles fool you, Princess. We are still demons. This is still a dangerous place. Especially for you right now."

My stomach growls and Baron's head pops up, looking around. "I just realized I'm not sure when I last ate."

Fen sits up and adjusts a lever on the side of the boat, steering it in a different direction. "You'll enjoy Zeb's realm."

"Why's that?"

"You'll see soon enough."

When we round a bend it's like we've gone to Greece. A rocky mountain protrudes from the shore and is dotted with houses and pavilions. At the very top is a castle with an open arena near it. It's a loud city, even at this time of night. People everywhere are drinking, laughing, eating, and indulging in carnal delights. The boat pulls into a small dock. Around us are other people in boats, though they don't seem to be traveling so much as relaxing. One couple smokes something that smells heady and musty. They look *quite* relaxed. Another couple is making out next to a picnic basket and wine. Seems vampires enjoy the night, even when they have the day.

Fen jumps out of the boat and offers me his hand. It's warm, strong, and I don't want to let go once I'm out. He doesn't seem to want to either, because we hold hands for several moments longer than necessary before someone bumps into us on the docks.

"Sorry about that!" The man laughs with his buddies and drunkenly saunters off in search of something else to entertain him.

"I take it Zeb is the Prince of Gluttony?"

"He is. And he provides the bulk of the food for our kingdom. Come, let's get you fed and get home."

I stay close to him as we walk through the town. It's crowded with finely dressed people who all look ready to party. Fen seems to know where he's going and leads us through winding streets up the mountain until my legs burn and I'm hungrier than ever. Finally we reach a tavern that doesn't look like much, but the smells emanating from it make my stomach rumble again.

When Fen walks in, the noise and chatter of the place dies down and they all turn to stare. It seems the Prince of War is recognizable on sight.

A woman with an apron tied around her waist approaches Fen, her painted lips bright and her eyes dropping to admire all aspects of Fenris. "My Prince, it's so good to see you. How might I serve you this evening?"

The woman doesn't even look at me. I might as well be invisible. She is ogling the prince so blatantly I'm almost embarrassed for her, except he doesn't seem to notice. "A table for two, Dora. And please let my brother know we're here."

She nods, golden ringlets of hair falling into her tan face. "Two?"

Fen puts an arm around my shoulder. The weight of it throws me off balance and I stiffen my back to remain standing straight. Baron stands between our legs, seeming to enjoy our proximity.

Dora frowns. "Of course. Let me find you a table."

"A private table," Fen says.

"A private table, then."

She escorts us to the back of the tavern, and as we disappear into shadows, the laughter and banter starts up again. We end up at a booth removed from the main dining area, tucked into a corner with candlelight and nothing else. I slide into one side and Fen sits opposite me. Baron crawls under the table and lies on top of our feet.

"Do they have menus or...?" I have no idea how demon taverns work.

"Not usually. I'll order for you." I'm about to protest, but he holds up a hand. "If that's okay?"

"Uh, sure. Nothing too spicy, though."

Dora comes back with large mugs of red liquid and places one before each of us. "Do you know what you'd like?" she asks.

"Two falafels, a greek salad, pita bread with hummus, and a chicken breast for Baron."

I raise an eyebrow at him. "So it doesn't just look like Greece then? Is this a replica or something?"

"Many of our foods and cultures are inspired by your world, mixed with new elements that are unique to us. It's technology we can't copy." He sips his red drink. "My people come from another world entirely, but we were cast out and banished here. We've worked hard to create a new kind of world, one where we are as free as we can be under the constraints of the curses placed on us."

"Is everyone here a vampire?" I ask.

"No. But many are. Some might look more monstrous because of their particular charms."

"Like the dungeon demon," I say.

Fen smiles. "Like him, yes. There's also a heavy population of Fae here. Many are Shades...mixed bloods, the byproduct of a Fae and vampire union."

"Aren't Shades like spirits or ghosts?"

He shrugs. "Mixed bloods have some freedoms, because of their vampire blood, but they are still under many restrictions, particularly in regards to their use of magic. They have little rights. They live in hell. What are they if not Shades?" He drinks again. "Then there are full Fae, Outlanders who are now slaves to their vampire masters here."

"That's awful."

"It's better than the alternative," he says, taking a drink from his glass.

"What's the alternative?"

"Execution."

I sniff at my drink. It's sweet, so I take a sip. A cascade of flavors washes over my tongue, first sweet, then a bit tangy, then sour. The aftertaste returns to sweet, and I feel an instant lightness in my body as my blood warms. "Is this alcoholic?"

He grins. "Not the way you're thinking, but it will have a similar effect. Drink cautiously."

It's so good I can't help but take another drink.

Dora brings us food and it looks as good as it smells. I dig in, eating voraciously. I didn't realize how hungry I truly was until now.

"It seems we've been starving you," Fen says.

"I just haven't eaten much since my mom got sick," I say between bites. "It seems my appetite is coming back with a vengeance."

I eat everything on my plate and then finish Fen's falafel, before I'm finally satisfied. Dora brings us a plate of little balls of deep fried pastry dough soaked in honey syrup and cinnamon.

"These are *loukoumades*," Fen says, picking one up and popping it into his mouth. "You'll like them."

He's right. The sweet, flaky treats practically melt in my mouth and I devour them quickly.

As I lick the last of the honey off my fingers, a man approaches us, and Fen rises to greet him. Baron shifts at our feet, a very low growl in his throat.

"Fen! It's good to see you. And you brought the girl. Oh my!"

I stand, hoping I got all the honey off my fingers and shake hands with the man. He's not as tall as Fen, but he's very handsome in a softer sort of way. He has large brown eyes, a shock of dark hair that flops about on his head, and a kind face. "It's nice to meet you," I say.

"And you," he says, covering my hand with his as we shake. "You're prettier than Asher indicated. I think he was trying to keep you to himself."

I snort. "I'm pretty sure I annoy him too much for that."

Zeb sits with us, turning to Fen. "I have information on the matter we discussed." His voice is quiet, and he glances at me.

"You may speak in front of her," say Fen. "After all, she will be Queen one day."

Zeb nods. "I had my alchemists look into the poison found in father's room. It's, well…it's not a poison at all." Fen's eyes go wide, and Zeb continues, his voice growing more animated. "Someone weakened our father, then killed him."

"There were no wounds," says Fen.

"None that we noticed. If we reexamine the body, perhaps we'll find a small gash. Maybe they used a small needle-like weapon or—"

"You would have our father dug out from his grave?"

Zeb shrugs. "I'd consider it. Ace is keen on the idea. Don't you want to figure out what happened?"

Fen looks down and sighs. "We'll have to take this before the others."

"Ace and I are already drafting the proposal," says Zeb, smiling. He clasps his brother on the shoulder.

Fen shrugs him off and signals his wolf to stand by him. "We have to go, Zeb. But the meal was great, as usual."

Zeb frowns. "So soon? I'd hoped you'd stay for drinks. Maybe more dessert later."

Fen shakes his head. "I need to get her settled into my place so I can get back to work."

"Right. We will find out who did this, you know. They will pay."

Fen nods, and we leave the tavern. I don't ask the question that's burning in me until we are back on the boat. "Why didn't you tell him you suspected one of the princes?"

The boat begins to glide through the water and Fen stays alert and focused until we are away from the city. It seems the canals have different paths depending on where you are going: direct paths to move through the realms quickly, and side paths to travel within them. We are back on a direct path when Fenris finally answers me. "Until I know who to trust, I have to be careful. You should too. I plan to find out the truth before our month is over, so you don't end up in the wrong hands, but if I fail, don't tell any of them what you've learned. It will only put you at greater risk."

The red drink we had is making me sleepy, and despite my best efforts to stay awake, sleep claims me. When I wake, we are slowing, having already arrived in Fen's realm. The sun is rising over the mountains, a large golden globe in the sky that doesn't seem to do much to warm the land we are now in. I hadn't noticed that the further we traveled the colder it got, but now I'm shivering and Fen hands me my cloak.

"Is it always this cold here?"

"No, we have four seasons. This is the beginning of winter. We haven't seen cold yet. But it's coming."

"So...is that when hell freezes over?"

The look he gives me is funnier than my lame joke and I can't help but laugh. He remains stoic, and I nudge him with my foot. "Oh come on, you know that was funny. Lighten up."

"I am the Prince of War. I do not 'lighten up'."

We climb out of the boat and hike up a winding stone path carved with glyphs reminiscent of the mark on Fen's wrist. Dark trees loom over us, and something shuffles in the shrubbery. A squirrel runs out from the darkness, cheeks stuffed with food. I say hello to the critter at my feet. Fen grumbles something about "squirrels" and "just meat". Baron licks his lips. In a second, the squirrel disappears back into a bush, leaving behind tiny prints in the snow. I chuckle, a slither of early morning sun hitting my face, and we move on. The forest begins to part, letting more light flow onto the steps. We reach a tall wooden gate, one sentinel on either side, clad in silver steel, wielding spears, their faces covered in white fur hoods. Large trees arch over the entrance to form a shaded path beyond the walls. When Baron walks up and scratches at the gate, the guards open for us.

The city beyond the walls is just waking up. There's a scent of freshly baked pastries and breads stirring on the air, and the sounds of stores opening and people greeting one another.

The castle is in the distance, beyond the city, a sharp and jagged extension of the mountains that surround the area, forming three of the fortress's four walls.

Waterfalls cascade down the sides of the peaks, pooling into ponds and lakes that line the outskirts. I hear them before I see them, feeling their deep rumbling. They give the air a clean, fresh scent.

We walk under the trees that stretch over us, and as the sun hits the bark, something catches my eye. I walk toward one of the trees and run my hand over it. The trunk of the tree, of all the trees, is embedded with crystals of all shapes and colors. My hand lands on one particular crystal that pulses with its own light, like a bursting star set aflame in opaque quartz.

"We call that a Shooting Star Crystal," Fen says from behind me. "Many of these crystals can also be found in your world, but that is one unique to ours. It's said that it brings great power to those who know how to wield it, and can bring out great power within one for whom it is trapped. Some say it's also the knowing eye of truth, seeing through falsehoods."

"It's lovely. Do you believe it's that powerful?"

He shrugs. "I don't fancy myself an expert on such things."

"Fen here is more a steel and brawn kind of guy," a woman's voice says.

I turn and find a tall, slim, graceful woman link arms with Fen. She is stunning, with long blue hair, striking silver eyes that are shaped almost like a cat's, and...pointed ears. She wipes a dirty hand on her leather apron and holds it out to me. "I'm Kayla, this oaf's sister. You must be Arianna."

His sister? I shake her hand, surprised at the strength in someone so petite. "Yes. It's nice to meet you."

I try not to stare at her ears, but clearly I'm failing, because she laughs and touches the tip of one. "I'm half Fae," she says, by way of explanation. "Our father had a dalliance with one of his slaves. My mother."

I nod, pretending to understand.

Fen puts his arm around his sister and grins. "Kayla here is the best blacksmith in the kingdom, and our official royal blacksmith at Stonehill," Fen explains. "Swords, knives, even jewelry. She's the best in all the realms."

"How fascinating," I say. "I'd love to see what you do sometime, if you don't mind."

"Not at all." Kayla tugs on her long blue braid, her eyes crinkling in genuine happiness. She points to a building not too far from us, where black smoke rises from it. "That's my forge. Stop by anytime."

Kayla turns to Fen, her smile slipping. "I came to let you know we need a larger supply of steel if you want so many swords prepared so quickly. I'm running low."

Fen nods. "I'll see to it you have what you need."

"Good enough." Kayla turns away from us, waving as she does, and heads back to her forge.

"So if you're a prince, does that make her—"

"A princess? No. She's a bastard. A Shade. Everything she has in this life she's had to work for." His eyes grow dark. "My father...my father did not treat her kindly."

I take his arm, hoping to cheer him. "Show me more of your city."

Fen walks us through the mountain paths. Many of the shop owners and people greet us, but Fen is so lost in his own thoughts, he ignores them. I frown, seeing how they turn away from him, disappointed. Fen needs to work on his people skills.

We arrive at a drawbridge that crosses a stream of water made by the many waterfalls, and we cross over, into the entrance of the castle. Up close it's even more beautiful, in a fierce, defiant kind of way.

"This is Stonehill Castle," Fen says, an edge of pride in his voice. "Your home for the next month."

I nod, staring at the castle, then I turn to him, a question on my mind from his talk with Kayla. "Fen, why do you need so many swords so quickly?"

"Because war is coming, and it's my job to be ready."

7

STONEHILL CASTLE
Fenris Vane

"Fen here is more a steel and brawn kind of guy."
—Kayla Windhelm

I walk forward and push open the large doors. A draft of snow and wind follow us in, and I close the gates behind us to preserve some warmth. But these stone walls stay cold, and we will not have heat until we arrive at the inner quarters.

"It's late," I say. "You probably want to sleep. I'll show you to your room. In the morning, I'll give you a proper tour if you'd like."

"Actually, I'd like the tour now," Arianna says. "I'll need to know my way around if I'm to live here."

I grunt.

"Unless of course you're too tired…"

"I'm never tired." I say.

She tosses a dark braid over her shoulder and turns her head to look at me, her lips so red, her eyes so bright. "Then show me around, Prince." She walks forward, down the great hall draped with crimson banners, my sigil, the white wolf, upon them. She starts to skip, and I wonder how she can be so carefree, with everything that has happened.

Who is this girl?

When I was assigned to protect her, I did my research, learned about her childhood and schooling. I thought I knew her, but now I see, I knew nothing at all. There is something…different about her. The feeling of danger has been buzzing in my blood since she entered my life. It is a distraction I do not need and should not have, but she is part of the puzzle, and so she must be protected. Even from myself, if that's what it takes.

"Come on slowpoke," Arianna says.

I walk forward slowly. I have lived long enough to know how to say no to temptations, but there is something about Arianna that pushes past my walls, and that is not safe for either of us.

Baron nudges against her leg, making puppy eyes. Even my traitorous wolf senses the difference in her. I wonder, would he turn on even me to protect her?

"Here." I motion to a door on the left. "This leads to the west wing. There you will find the kitchens and storage rooms. In the east wing, you will find the servants quarters."

"And is this your throne?" Arianna climbs the few steps at the end of the hall and sits down on the chair, a massive thing carved from grey stone, a red banner draped over the back. "Fancy."

There are only a few servants awake at this hour, but they all freeze and stare at the princess. She doesn't seem to notice, or perhaps she just doesn't care. "It's my least favorite part of the castle," I say, walking up to her. "But it is useful when one needs to appear powerful, when one must enforce the laws of the land."

She swallows, the smile slipping from her lips. I can't bring myself to regret intervening when Dean threw his charms at her. But it was foolish nonetheless. I have an investigation to mount, a murderer to capture, and a kingdom to save from the brink of war. I do not have time for this.

"Show me your favorite part," she says.

Despite myself, I smile and guide her to the center of the hall, under the wooden archway. Once we pass, she looks up. "It's a tree," she says, placing a hand on the bark.

I lead her to the side, up a staircase that winds around the trunk and past branches. Different paths sprout out from our own, leading to different rooms and levels. "This tree grows through the center of the castle," I say, pointing to the leaves glowing with yellow light. "This is my favorite part."

She stands still, her mouth agape.

"I know it's not what people expect when they hear Prince of War, but—"

"It's amazing," she says.

I smile, glad she is pleased with what will be her home for a month. Maybe even longer...

No. I will not think of that.

My lips twitch and she smiles. Guilelessly. Beautifully. Like we share a secret no one else knows.

But I'm the only one with secrets.

And she can never know them.

I turn away. "You would think, from the outside looking in, that the interior would be dark and gloomy, but I had windows carved into brick throughout. Some clear, some stained glass, and it gives color and light to the nooks and crevices."

She looks around thoughtfully, a small frown on her face. I broke the moment between us, but it is the way things must be.

She follows me with light steps up a path to the second level. I can smell her, and it's a scent I find hard to resist. Sweet and spicy, just like her.

We stop in front of a wooden door carved with eagles. "This is your room. I had your staff prepare it for you, so it should have everything you need. But if not, the women who serve you occupy rooms downstairs, and you can summon them with a bell by your bed. They can get you anything you require to make your stay more comfortable."

"Where do you sleep?" she asks. Her eyes seem to dig into my soul, prying it open.

"I'm in the room down the hall." I point to another door, this one decorated with a wolf. "If you need anything."

"Okay. Thanks. I guess I'll see you in the morning." Her hand rests on the doorknob, and she looks at me questioningly.

"Did you need something else, Arianna?"

"Just Ari. And, actually yes. I have two favors to ask."

"And they would be?"

Her eyes dart from mine to her hands as she fidgets with the blue sandstone ring she always wears. "I'd like a sword."

It was not what I was expecting. "Do you know how to use one?"

She shakes her head. "No, and that's my second favor. I want you to teach me."

...

The fire in my room is already lit when I enter, and I stand in front of my bed. I'm not sure I'm ready to sleep, though it is late and I haven't slept in three days.

It is a myth that my kind do not need sleep. We just need less of it and for different reasons.

Arianna wouldn't let me leave until I promised to do as she asked. I don't have time to play teacher to a novice, though I must admit her desire to learn is encouraging. And perhaps it will help keep her safe.

Baron trudges into the room after me. "She finally tell you to go?" I ask.

The wolf lies down in front of the fireplace, with something akin to a smile on his face. Ari had tried nudging him in my direction with no success a few minutes ago. She acted contrite about it, but I saw the smirk.

"You know," I say, "I'd feel a lot better about the whole thing if you'd just snarl at her like you do at everyone else."

She sighs. Then snores.

I strip off my clothes and head to the bathroom. Since we cannot use modern technology, we have had to find creative ways of making magic work for us. My washroom includes a bathtub that fills up with fresh water and heats itself using magic. The toilet is simple, an ancient design that drains waste into a sewage system. The sink uses water from the mountains. The shower is the best thing my brother, Ace, has ever invented. Next to a large window that overlooks the mountains a small waterfall sprouts from the wall.

Magic heats the pipes built into the castle. I step onto the stone and let the water wash over me, pounding into my tired muscles until I feel clean and more relaxed. When I exit the washroom, Ari is there, sitting at the small table by the fireplace. She stands, her eyes wide when she sees me standing there naked, holding my towel. "Oh, crap, I'm so sorry. I was just...I thought I would wait...I didn't..."

She can't seem to finish her sentences, but she's not averting her eyes either. I don't bother covering myself. We are not modest creatures by nature, and I certainly have nothing to hide.

I'm not sure what I'm expecting from her. A demure shifting of her eyes? A blush? I get neither. Instead she takes her time looking at me, and then she smiles. "It seems only fair, since you saw me naked while I was unconscious."

"If we're being fair, I also had to touch you." I want to see how far she'll take this. But I realize I'm not prepared for her to walk over to me and lay her small hands on my chest. Her body is so close, but not quite touching mine. My muscles flex as I resist the urge to grab her and pull her closer, to bury my teeth in her neck and feel her life pulse into me. There are so many things I would love to do to this innocent creature standing before me, but instead I suck in my breath and wait to see what she does next.

Her hands glide over my chest, feeling their way over my muscles, down to my abs. She stops at my hips and I nearly groan. My body is making my feelings clear, but I can't read her face.

The air between us is thick with unmet desire, but instead of giving in, she steps away. "I assume you didn't actually fondle me when you changed me. Did you?" There is a challenge in her startling green eyes.

"No, I didn't." My voice is thick, deeper than normal.

"Then we're even."

She returns to the table and sinks into the chair. I'm nearly shaking with need, but I push it aside and reach for my pants, pulling them on as quickly as I can despite their discomfort at the moment. "Might I inquire as to why you are here, in my room, in the middle of the night?"

For the first time since I found her here, she drops her eyes, as if embarrassed. "You'll think it's stupid."

I pull out a bottle of brandy I keep for emergency emotional occasions, and I pour us each a drink, then sit across from her. "Try me," I say, sipping the drink.

There's a waver in her voice when she speaks, and it nearly breaks me.

"Twice now someone has tried to kidnap or kill me. In my world and now here. I...I've never been attacked before. I've never felt unsafe in my whole life. I've felt hungry, broke, even scared. But it was poverty that was the enemy, not real flesh and blood villains. I always thought I was strong, that I could handle anything, but I'm starting to think I was wrong." She looks up now, straight into my eyes. "Fen, I'm scared. I'm scared to be alone. I know that makes me pathetically weak, but it's the truth. I can't sleep. Can't even close my eyes because I keep seeing these faceless monsters attacking me." A single tear falls from one eye down her cheek.

I ignore my own warnings and lift a finger to her jaw to wipe the tear away. "You're safe here. I will protect you."

Baron is already at her feet, but he lifts his head and lays it on her lap. "Apparently, so will he," I say.

She sniffles, smiles and straightens her spine. "Thanks. Sorry to go all weepy on you the very first night. I'm sure princesses and queens aren't supposed to do things like this."

I shrug. "I have no idea. We haven't had either since our mother was killed many, many years ago."

She tilts her head. "You had a mother?"

I laugh. "I didn't spontaneously appear, if that's what you mean."

"I guess I don't know what I mean." She twirls a loose strand of hair in her fingers as she talks. "You're a demon. I didn't imagine demons procreating and being birthed into the world. I suppose I imagined it more like some Being—like God—creating you all fully formed. Like fallen angels and all the Bible stuff I learned as a kid."

"Your 'Bible stuff' is more like myths and partial truths based on some semblance of what happened. Vaguely. A very long time ago, we were part of another world, as I mentioned earlier. Our people were unified, but the king of that realm began making choices that his brother did not agree with. They fought, and the brother lost and was cast out, along with all those who supported the uprising. That's when our kind came here, to this world. But the king didn't stop at exile. He cursed them all, and their ancestors, so that we'd become the demons we are now. Vampires, driven by bloodlust, needing humans to survive but having a fatal weakness in the human world. It was the king's ultimate revenge for what he saw as betrayal." It feels strange talking to someone from earth about all this, but soon enough she will take the Blood Oath and become one of us. I hate imagining that, imagining her cursed with our thirst, with our weaknesses, with our damnation, just to save her mother.

She yawns and her eyelids droop. I realize she must be exhausted. I'm about to suggest she go back to her room and get some sleep, but I remember she said she can't sleep. And so I do my second very unwise thing of the night. I offer to let her sleep in my room.

With me.

I expect her to refuse. Maybe part of me even hopes she does. But she doesn't. Instead, she crawls into my large bed and takes a side, as if she belongs there. She pats the other side. "I'm not going to kick you out of your bed. We slept together once, technically. We can do it again." Baron jumps onto the bed with her and she scratches behind his ear. "Besides, I think he'll put up a fight if you try anything while I'm asleep."

I half expect she's right about that. I'm glad Baron's looking out for her, because though I swore to protect her, I might not always be around.

Normally I sleep naked, but tonight I keep my pants on and slide under the covers. Her body is covered only in a thin cotton gown, and though it is a big bed, she is not on the edge. I can feel her skin against mine. Her shape curving in closer to me as she settles in to sleep.

I lay there for an hour or so before her breathing finally steadies and I know she is asleep. Even then I cannot follow easily. There is too much temptation to touch her, to hold her, and having her so close but not quite close enough is a sweet kind of torture I am unused to.

At some point, though, my body takes over, and I finally drift.

...

My arm is around her, and her body is pressed against mine when I awaken aroused and thirsty. My mouth is at her throat, her vein pulsing under pale delicate skin. It would be so easy to sink my teeth into her. And it is so hard to release her and pull myself out of bed. I allowed myself to sleep too long and now I am behind.

I use the washroom and dress for the day. As I pull on my boots, Ari sits up in bed. "What time is it?" she asks.

"Well past dawn," I tell her. I know she wants an hour and minute, like in her world, but we do not track time in the same way.

She climbs out of bed and stretches. "Thank you for letting me stay here last night."

Baron, who slept by her side all night, springs out of bed and paces the room. He needs to be let out to run, to hunt. And I need to feed. It has been too long and I can feel the bloodlust building in me. Sleeping with Arianna only made it worse.

"It was no trouble," I say. A small lie. "Get dressed and we'll eat. Then I have work to do. In a few days, I'll need to head back to High Castle."

She frowns at my words. "Why?"

"I need to continue the investigation into my father's death."

"Don't forget you also promised to teach me how to sword fight."

"I haven't forgotten," I say. "When I can't be with you, I'm going to leave Baron and two guards I trust to make sure you're safe."

She nods and leaves the room, and the space feels too empty without her.

While she's changing, I take Baron to the woods outside the city. I need to chase something, to catch prey and drain its blood. I need to feed before my cravings overcome me. I can't afford any weakness while Arianna is here. Until she is gone for good, I must remain in control.

The sun is high in the sky and the air is cool but not frigid. We still have a fortnight at least before the coldest part of winter sets in. "Ready to hunt, boy?"

Baron raises his head to the sky and howls. I am faster than my wolf, but I pace myself to keep stride with him. It's better to run with him than alone. Blood pumps through my body, invigorating my senses. Everything around me is heightened. The scent of the lingering snow on the ground, the crunch of branches underfoot, the insects swarming deep undercover of brush and bark, the critters scampering through trees and bushes to get out of the way of the predators they sense coming into their world.

There are small creatures we could hunt, but I need something larger. Something that will put up a fight. So we go deeper into the woods, running so fast, so far, that I can no longer see Stonehill. It is then that I smell what I'm after. A black bear.

Baron backs away, uncertain, but he knows I'll watch his back, so he follows. I tear through the trees until I see the bear emerging from a cave. It shouldn't be so close to the village. It's a risk to my people. These are my justifications as I throw myself at the beast, teeth extended, power surging, and end its life.

After my blood lust is quenched—as quenched as it can be on animal blood and not human—I sit on a rock in the sun as Baron hunts smaller prey. He's content with his rabbit for breakfast, and then we return to Stonehill.

...

Ari is already sitting at the dining table when we arrive. Baron rushes to lie at her feet, and she pets his head with affection. I sit across from her.

She's dressed for a day of training in pants and a form-fitting tunic. Her hair is pulled back in braids.

Once I'm sitting, Olga, the cook, brings in plates for us both. She's been in my service for many years and knows the routine of this house instinctually. Though she looks to be in her early 30s, she is actually an immortal Fae. Her pointed ears attest to that, which at the moment are prominently displayed over the white hair that is pulled back in a bun.

"Thank you, Olga," Ari says. "This looks delicious."

Olga smiles. "You're welcome. I added extra apple dumpling since you seemed so taken with it."

When Ari smiles her whole face lights up. "Wonderful. I can't wait to learn how to prepare it myself."

Olga pats her hand. "Not that you should ever need to, Your Highness."

When Olga leaves, I stare at the girl across from me. "What was that about?"

She shrugs, spooning the porridge and apple dumpling into her mouth and taking her time to chew before answering. "I got bored waiting for you, so I introduced myself to the kitchen staff and offered to help. Actually, I had to insist since they wouldn't let me. I'm afraid I created quite a scandal, but I do plan on repeating the experience." She raises a spoon with more apple dumpling. "I must learn how to make this. It's amazing."

I shake my head as I take my own spoonful. It's odd, seeing someone ranked so high take such a personal interest in the servants. She definitely does not behave the way royalty here are used to. "I've a feeling you'll be creating quite a few scandals while you're here."

She grins. "Here's hoping."

...

I take her to the outside training arena after breakfast and hand her a wooden sword. "We start with this."

She frowns at it. "Seriously? I'm not a child. This looks like a toy."

There are others out here training. Some are my soldiers staying in battle shape. Others are children just learning their sword. I whistle to one of the soldiers. "Marco, come."

Marco jogs over. He's about my height, with slightly less bulk, but he's strong and trained well. I trained him myself, so I should know. I toss him a wooden sword and take up one myself. "The Princess here thinks these are toys. Care to help me demonstrate what they can do?"

Marco grins. "Yes, sir."

I don't hold back. Much. If I put my full power into the fight I'd break both swords and probably Marco as well. He throws himself into the fight, though. Ari watches wide-eyed as we circle one another in the yard, parrying blows and attempting to strike each other. A few others stop to watch, so we put on a show. In the end, I disarm Marco and pin him to the ground with my sword. I look over at Ari. "If I was trying to hurt him, I could kill him with this thing you call a toy. It just wouldn't kill as easily or as fast as one made of metal, which is the point. Until you learn control and technique, I can't risk you using a sharpened steel sword. But once you're ready, we'll have one made for you."

Her eyes light up at that. "Okay, I get it. Teach me."

I nod to Marco. "Pick one of your best men. I'm putting you and him on guard duty for the moment, until the threat to the Princess's life passes."

Marco nods sharply, sparing a glance for Arianna, who is studying the practice swords. "Yes, sir. We won't let any harm come to the Princess."

A low growl forms in my throat. "See that you don't."

He is dismissed, and I begin training Ari.

We move through basic stance positions, strikes and defenses. I show her the proper way to hold a sword. She learns fast.

"Widen your stance," I say.

She does.

"Spin your torso when you strike. No. Like this." I stand behind her and lay my hands on her hips. I twist them back, then forward.

She smiles, her cheeks red. "I think I got it. How do you—"

"Your Highness," someone yells. A kid, no older than ten and four years. He can barely speak when he approaches me, so out of breath is he. "I...I have a message...I—"

"Calm yourself, boy. The words won't come if sharing space with so much air."

He nods, takes a few deep, slow breaths, and speaks again. "Sir, you're needed at the southern lumber mill.

One of Prince Ace's contraptions malfunctioned. A man was injured. The rest are refusing to work."

"Bloody hell. Can't Henrick handle this?"

The boy shakes his head. "Henrick is the one who got hurt, Sir."

"All right. Tell the stable to ready my horse. I'll be there shortly."

"Two horses," Ari says from beside me. "Have the stable master ready two horses please, uh, I didn't catch your name?"

The boy looks at Arianna and his cheeks burn red. He stutters now more than before. "Um. My name? It's, uh. John. My name is John, Your, er, Majesty Highness."

Ari holds her hand out to him. "Hi John, I'm Ari. Thanks so much for rushing to get this message here. You did a good job. After you speak to the stable master, hop over to the kitchen and tell Olga I said you should have some tea and cookies before you're sent back, okay?"

I raise an eyebrow at Ari, but I don't contradict her, at least not in front of everyone who is watching.

John looks to me, uncertain how to proceed with such odd orders. I just nod. "Do as the Princess says, boy. And be quick about it."

He nods, his face breaking into a smile, and runs to the stables.

I turn to Ari. "What was that about?"

She puts a hand on my arm. "You catch more flies with honey than vinegar, Fen. Didn't anyone ever teach you that?"

She's already walking towards the stables, and I jog to catch up, grumbling under my breath about flies. Who needs flies anyways?

8

SEALED IN BLOOD

"You've never seen me fight."
—Fenris Vane

I can hear Fen mumbling his complaints. I ignore them. Olga had little to say about her master, but her silence told me enough. Fen's servants respect him, but they don't care for him. I see it in the way they stare at him when he's not looking, at the way they avert their gaze under his glare. Most of them are Fae. Slaves. It makes me want to hate Fen and his brothers. But, somehow, I don't.

I don't hate him. I find him frustrating and exasperating, but also...fascinating. There is a kind heart in there somewhere. I saw it last night when he let me sleep in his room, though I could tell he didn't want me to. I saw it the night he saved me back in my world, and then stayed all night watching movies with me. I see it in the way he treats Baron, and in the way he cares about his brothers.

There's good in him. I just need to nudge it out. Help him show these people he actually does care about them and their welfare.

When we arrive at the stables behind the castle, two horses are already prepared for us. This might be a good time to admit to Fen that I've never ridden a horse before. But I'm afraid he'll make me stay behind, so I don't tell him. I just watch as he mounts and try to copy what he does. I've seen movies. I know the gist. It can't be that hard, right?

My horse is beautiful. She's black with a white marking on her forehead, and her eyes stare at me with such wisdom. I do manage to make it onto her without falling on my ass. I pat my horse's neck. "What's her name?" I ask the stable master.

She's a stout woman with pointy ears and long sand colored hair that pulls into a tail at the base of her neck. Her face is wide and leathery and she looks like she's been living with these horses for all of eternity. "She's Diamond, and she should serve you well, Your Highness. The Prince picked her out for you himself."

I look over at Fen, surprised. "You did?"

He grunts. "I knew you would need something on which to get around."

"Thank you. She's amazing."

The stable master nods with approval. "That she is. She'll treat you good if you do her right."

Baron follows us as we walk our horses for a bit. I think I'm getting the hang of it, but I'm nervous that if Diamond starts to trot or run I'll lose control.

"I'm surprised the horses aren't spooked by Baron," I say, pulling Diamond up to the side of Fen and his horse.

"They've become acclimated to him, and he to them. It's an uneasy alliance, but it works." He takes us down to a dirt road and turns to me. "Are you ready to run? We need to get there fast."

I swallow, regretting my decision not to tell him about my lack of experience. But it's too late now. "Sure, let's do it."

He grins and makes a clicking sound, gently nudging his horse on the side. He picks up speed, so I copy him and Diamond begins to trot, then run. I grip her body with my knees, my knuckles holding on to the leather strap so hard I fear I'll break it. But I don't fall off. We ride fast down the path and through the woods until I begin to hear the sounds of people. Fen slows to a trot, then a walk as we reach a lumberyard. An area of trees has been cleared and piles of trunks line the grass. A machine that reminds me of a giant pizza cutter sits in the center, covered in black smoke. Men are scattered throughout the clearing, talking, pacing, drinking. Not working. There are no women, which I find odd. In fact, there are only male vampires, from what I can tell. Not a Fae or Shade amongst them.

They all turn in unison to face us, and I try not to embarrass myself as I dismount Diamond. "Thanks girl," I whisper into her ear. "You made me look good. I owe you a treat when we get back."

Fen, who apparently overheard me, gives me a lopsided grin and hands me an apple. I hold it out to Diamond, who wraps her large, soft horse lips around it and chomps it up.

A big, brawny man in flannel with a bushy red beard stomps up to Fen, two men flanking him. He's frowning. "We're done!" he says. "No man can work in conditions like this."

Fen crosses his arms over his chest. "You're not exactly men, are you?"

The man glares. "No demon neither."

"Where is Henrick?" Fen asks.

"I'm over here, Sir."

We both turn in the direction of the voice. Henrick lies on a wooden table under a tarp, his leg propped up and bandaged. His hair is dark brown and a black tattoo covers half his neck. Fen strides over to him. "What happened?"

"The wood cutter jammed. When I tried to clear it, the damn thing exploded on me. My leg is pretty ripped up."

"We'll get you patched up." Fen signals to several of the men standing around. "Take him to Navia in Stonehill. Tell her I sent you. He's to receive the best care, understood?"

"Yes, Sir," the men say.

"I'm sorry, Sir," Henrick says. He's far too pale and his jaw clenches in pain as he tries to talk. "We were already behind in production. There's no way we'll make the deadline before winter hits."

Fen nods sharply, but offers no other words. I walk over and lay a hand on Henrick's. "Just take care of yourself and heal. The rest will sort itself out. It always does."

Henrick looks startled by my touch. For that matter, so does Fen, but once again he chooses not to contradict me in front of others. Interesting. I'm sure we'll have a lively conversation about things later, once we're alone.

Just thinking about being alone with him makes my skin hot. I played it cool, acting like seeing him naked and touching his body didn't affect me. But lord, that was my biggest lie ever told. I can't get the image of that man out of my head. Or the feel of him off my skin. His scent alone makes me want things I shouldn't want. I still have to live with six other princes. I can't fall for Fen, not now. And besides, he's made it clear he has no desire to be King. He doesn't even want me to pick him.

I'm setting myself up for heartbreak if I give my heart to a man who doesn't want it.

The men place Henrick on a cot on wheels and attach it to a horse, then begin guiding him slowly to town.

Fen faces those who remain. "We have a fortnight or two until winter hits. Once that happens, we will not be able to harvest trees until spring thaws the land. This wood needs to be used for fire, heat, cooking, and building, throughout the entire kingdom. It is our primary export. If we don't meet our quota, people everywhere will suffer. Now get back to work and make it happen. I'll take a look at the machine, but if I can't fix it right now, then cut and sort wood by hand like we did before my brother invented the cutter. In the meantime, I'll talk to Ace about potential design flaws."

There are grumbles as Fen walks over to the machine in question. A few men return to their work, using axes to cut the tree trunks into splintered wood or smaller logs. But the men who originally confronted Fen stand and glare at him as he works on the machine. I turn away to scan the rest of the clearing, walking amongst the logs that are piled and ready for distribution, and the trees still needing to be cut. The scent of pine and freshly cut wood fills the air, mixed with something more vinegar-like.

Sunlight filters through the tall canopies of the trees and I walk towards the woods, away from the repetitive sounds of steel hitting wood: chop chop chop. Towards the sound of running water. I'm hoping to find a stream where I can wait while Fen does his work. Something about those men makes me uneasy, and I'm beginning to regret coming with him, but it's important I know what kind of work this realm does. If I'm stuck here for all eternity, I'm going to make it work for me, which means making it better.

My dreams of being a lawyer and helping people that way might be over, but that doesn't mean I can't still affect change in the lives of those around me. And that's just what I intend to do, whether the princes of hell like it or not.

After a bit of searching, I find the stream. I can still hear the men working, but water trickling over rocks muffles the sound. I sit on a boulder in the shade of a sad looking willow tree whose branches extend over the river, dipping into it.

I watch a small red bird jump from rock to rock. This place is peaceful, serene, and—

A branch snaps behind me.

I spin around to face the intruder. It's the man with the red beard and flannel. The man who looked so angry at Fen when we arrived.

I stand and step back as he approaches me, his body invading my space as he breathes into my face. His breath smells of alcohol and his eyes roam over my body in a way that makes my skin crawl. "So you're the little bitch they brought to decide everyone's fate? What makes you so special, huh?" He brings his dirty hand to my face and grabs my chin so hard it hurts.

I shove his chest, but he doesn't budge. Of course not. He's a demon. A vampire. Strong. Too strong for me. "Get your hands off me," I hiss at him through clenched teeth. "You will not like what happens if you don't."

"Oh? What are you going to do? Tell the big, bad prince on me? You don't know who my family is, do you?"

He leans in close to my face and extends his sharp fangs, then sticks out his tongue and runs it over my cheek. "Do you taste as good as you smell, I wonder?"

I try to fight him off, but he pins me against the willow tree, his thick, sweaty body pressing against me until I can't breathe. His teeth slide along my neck, nearly piercing my skin.

I have no weapon, so I pull a branch off the tree and swing it at him, hitting him in the head.

His teeth are no longer at my neck, but his grip tightens around my arm. He looks much angrier than he did before. A bear riled from his sleep.

So I do what I've always been taught to do when under attack by a stranger. I scream. I scream so loud the man looks shocked. He squeezes my neck hard and slams my head against the tree. I hit with a painful thud, tripping over a branch, falling towards the water.

The man has a choice. Hold onto my neck and join me in the water, or let go. He lets go, but looks ready to follow, when a wolf growls from the top of a boulder behind him.

Baron jumps onto my attacker.

He bites him in the shoulder.

I scramble away, splashing out of the water, my heart pounding, my hands shaking. Baron pins the man down, his wolf teeth at the man's throat. I stand in the mud. "Doesn't feel so good having a predator at your throat, does it?" I ask.

Fen arrives a moment later and quickly takes in the scene. "What is going on here?" He's not asking me, he's asking the man pinned by Baron. "What did you do to the Princess?"

"I didn't do nothing! I swear!" The man is a mix of anger and panic. "Was just having a nice chat with the Princess when this beast attacked me for no reason."

Fen places a foot on the man's arm and presses in. Bones snap. A scream fills the air.

"Let's try this again," Fen says. "What did you do, Rodrigo?"

"She just smelled so good. You don't let us feed neither. Not proper-like. And I was thirsty!"

Baron growls again and Fen looks like he's about to lose his shit. This time I don't intervene or play nice.

This time I want blood. Justice. Maybe vengeance. Something. I'm sick of men acting like they are entitled to the bodies of women just because they want them. I'm sick of this mentality, regardless of which world it's on. So I don't try to temper Fen's rage. Not with Rodrigo. I want the prince to unleash his own brand of wrath.

Fen lifts Rodrigo by his neck and Baron jumps off the man's chest, snapping at him just in case he forgets who's in charge. Then Fen drags Rodrigo through the woods, back to the center of the clearing where the other men wait. I follow, watching as my attacker attempts to get away from Fen, who doesn't seem to even break a sweat keeping hold of the bulky demon.

When we arrive, I see the cutter is working again, diligently chopping logs into smaller and smaller piles.

Fen throws the man into the center of the field. "Rodrigo seems to believe you are not being cared for properly. That my laws about feeding are too strict, that he is entitled to drink from the Princess *against her will*. Are any of you in agreement?"

All the men take a step back and look down at their feet, even the two who had stood by Rodrigo's side earlier.

"Very well, then we have just one traitor to deal with. Normally, I would sentence him to immediate execution for such an act against royalty. But I'm feel-ing generous today. So instead, I make his punishment a duel. To the death. Whichever one of us is left stand-ing at the end, wins."

What? No, this isn't what I wanted. I tug at Fen's arm to get his attention. "Can I talk to you privately?"

He nods, then turns to the group. "Don't let him leave, or it'll be your head."

We walk far enough away that I hope others can't hear us. "You can't fight him to the death!" I say.

He chuckles. "Why not?"

"What if you get hurt?"

Now he laughs. "You think he has any chance against me? That's sweet, but you've clearly never seen me fight."

"I've seen you fight a few times actually. Things can go wrong."

He brushes a strand of hair from my face and smiles. "You've seen me spar. You've seen me battle while you were drugged and nearly unconscious. You've never seen me fight. I'll be fine. No one touches you like that and walks away." He heads back to the waiting men, and I follow him, my heart hammering in my chest.

Baron stands by my side, his head under my hand, as the two men take up their swords and face each other.

"My father will hear about this," Rodrigo says as they circle each other.

"Your father owes more than his weight in gam-bling debts. And I own the note on those. He will not raise so much as an eyebrow at me. Now fight."

Rodrigo lunges. Fen counters. The whole thing is over so fast I almost think I lost time. It was no fight at all, but a slaughter. Rodrigo's body lies on the ground, his blood seeping into the dirt, his head a few feet from his torso, staring blindly into space.

In one move, Fen beheaded the man with no effort.

...

I'm quiet on the ride back to the castle and excuse myself to my room once we return. I wanted blood and I got it, but it didn't make me feel better. Instead, I feel sick. Sick of the violence and the attempts on my life. Sick of the games. I just need a break.

In truth, I want to go home. I want to check on my mom and sit on my old couch and see my best friends. I want to have a coffee and check my email and text and watch cat videos on Facebook. This world is so archaic. I feel lost. Alone.

When I get to my room, Julian and Kara are already there, cleaning and checking the fire. They both curtsy when I come in.

"We didn't think you'd be back yet," Julian says, by way of apology. "We will come back later." She drops her eyes and waits. She acts demure. Subservient. But I sense more within her. She's a petite girl with green eyes like mine and bright red hair. She reminds me of my mother in some ways.

Kara is taller, with a curvy figure and long golden hair with dark eyes. She always looks bored, but I think she plots more than she lets on.

They are both Fae, assigned to be my servants. Their pointy ears give it away, but I think I would know even without them.

"Don't go," I say. "Sit with me and have some tea. I could use the company."

There's a knock at the door and I open it to see Baron waiting beside Marco, the soldier Fen sparred with earlier. He's with another man. "Your Highness, the Prince asked us to stand watch. This is Roco. He and I will take shifts guarding you while you live here. If you need anything, please let one of us know. There will always be someone standing guard outside your door at all times, or with you when you move about the castle."

Baron pushes past my legs to walk in, and Marco's eyes widen. "Also, Fen said Baron will be staying with you from now on, except during hunts."

I nod and pat the wolf's head. "Very well. Thank you both."

Marco bows and closes the door, leaving me with my servants and the wolf. The girls are both wide-eyed and standing in the corner, as far away from Baron as they can. He just ignores them and hops onto my bed to sleep.

"Doesn't it scare you to have that wolf in here?" Kara asks.

"No, Baron would never hurt me. In fact, he protected me today." I tell them both the story of what happened as we move into my sitting room and Kara serves everyone tea.

When I'm done, Julian covers her mouth in shock. "You don't know who Rodrigo is, do you?"

"Honestly, I don't know who anyone is yet." Not even myself, in this crazy place.

"He's the son of the highest ranking demon in all the realms, outside the princes themselves," Julian says. "He was the Head Advisor to the King, before His Majesty was killed, and is responsible for enacting all the King's rulings. I can't believe the Prince killed his son."

"Fen mentioned something about gambling debts the father owed?"

Julian shrugs. "There are rumors, but the Prince would know better than us."

I sense Julian isn't telling me everything she knows, but then, why should she? She's a slave. We can sit here acting like friends, but at the end of the day she has no rights.

Kara shakes her head. "I can't believe that bastard tried to feed on you. But even still, the punishment was harsh for one of his ranking. His father won't take this lightly."

"Why was he working as lumber jack if he's so high ranking?" I ask.

"The King ordered him sent here to work 'a hard day's labor' for one year and one day, following an incident at a tavern with a local girl who ended up being favored by a nobleman," Kara explains. "It was his punishment, in hopes of teaching him some values."

"I don't think the lesson took," I say.

We spend the rest of the afternoon talking about our lives, our families and how different our experiences have been. Both Kara and Julian are slaves, taken as part of the spoils of war when their village from the Outlands tried to attack Fen's city. Normally their sentence would have been death, so they both seem happy to at least be alive. But still, they have no freedom, no pay, no choices at all.

"Were you part of the attack?" I ask.

Kara shakes her head. "We were too young at the time. We were taken when the demons retaliated on our village. To be honest, we have lived in this castle most of our lives. It's really all we've known."

"What does your contract say, exactly?" I ask, my mind whirring with ideas.

Julian frowns. "I haven't looked at it in ages. But I can get it for you if you'd like to see it. I think you technically own the contract now that we've been given to you."

"What? I own you?" My stomach turns on itself. How could Fen make me a slave-owner without telling me?

They both nod.

"Get me both of your contracts, at once."

They leave to do as I've asked, and I go back to my bedroom and crawl into the bed with the wolf, laying my head on his body. "What am I doing here, Baron? Do you have any clue?"

...

My day passes with some reading, some journaling and more talking with Kara and Julian about their contracts. I'm still trying to understand all the nuances of their terms. The language and style of writing is more obscure than the legalese of my world, and that's saying something. I might need to get help with this. When the dinner bell rings I realize I've skipped lunch entirely.

Fen waits for me at the dining table, and I take my seat across from him. There is an awkward silence between us as Olga brings out baked duck with salad, garlic rolls and fried vegetables.

I eat quickly, wondering the whole time what I will do each and every day in this new place. I have no real job now, and I guess I don't really need one. But I need some purpose. Some direction.

"Fen?"

He looks up, surprised I broke the silence. "Yes?"

"Thank you for defending me today. I know it will cause some problems for you to have killed someone with such a high ranking father. So, thank you."

His eyes soften. "I thought you were angry with me."

I shrug. "No. I wanted him to die. I was just surprised at the violence. And the blood." I shiver at the memory. "But this isn't my world anymore, is it? I have to adapt to this culture if I'm going to make it here."

He nods. "That you will."

"About the girls you assigned to me. Kara and Julian?"

"Are they not working out? Would you like someone different?" he asks.

"No, they're great. I was just wondering...do I own them? Is that how this works?"

He puts his fork down and looks at me more closely. "Technically, yes. I know you find that distasteful, given where you're from and the values you were raised with. But here it is the way things have always been."

"So I own their contract then?"

He frowns. "Yes," he says carefully. "But that contract was sealed in blood. Even you cannot break it. Just as we could not break your mother's contract once it was secured."

"I understand. Thank you."

I take another bite and he just looks at me, likely wondering what I'm up to now. He'll find out soon enough.

9

FINDING PURPOSE

*"A princess? No. She's a bastard. A Shade. Everything
she has in this life she's had to work for. My father...
my father did not treat her kindly."*

—Fenris Vane

I may not be able to break the contract, but I'm determined to improve it. I train late into the night with Fen, then wake early and finish breakfast before he and Baron return from their morning hunt. I'm leaving just as he arrives.

"You look to be in a rush," he says, when I nearly slam into him as he enters the dining hall.

"Just have some research I want to do," I say vaguely. I don't want to tell him my plan yet, because I don't want him to try to talk me out of it.

"Anything I can help with?" He raises an eyebrow, clearly curious about my intentions.

"Nope. I'll be in the library most of the day if you need me." He's standing so close to me I can smell him. I want to step back, to clear my head from the influence he has on me, but I don't. Instead, I step closer and lay my hand on his chest, pointing to a spot on his shirt. "Blood?"

He looks down and frowns. "Apologies. I'm usually more careful."

"Fen, yesterday when Rodrigo attacked me. He said something about how you don't let them feed properly. What did he mean?" I'd been thinking a lot about the hierarchal structure here with the different races, and some questions were starting to pop up. Like how did the vampires get their human blood?

"My realm is stricter than others about feeding on humans. It causes some...unrest." He averts his eyes and I can tell we are dancing on a sore subject.

"Do you feed on humans?" The thought of him doing so does not settle well with me.

"When I must." He steps back. "But I limit the frequency of trips to your world for feeding, and I've curtailed the keeping of more than a minimum number of human slaves in our world."

"There are human slaves here? For feeding on?" This is the first I've heard of that.

"Not many, and nearly none in Stonehill. My brothers aren't as particular. Weren't you in a hurry to get to the library?"

Feeling summarily dismissed I nod and wish him a good morning before leaving. Baron follows me, and I hear my two guards trailing far enough behind me that I don't feel totally stalked.

I explore the castle looking for the library. I could just ask Marco or Roco for directions, but I'd rather find it on my own and see what else I discover in the process.

Sadly, I do not find any secret passages or exciting rooms full of treasures. I do, however, find a room full of dusty furniture and rugs that look like they haven't been moved since the dawn of time. I also find several empty chambers, that Marco informed me had been empty as long as he could remember. "The Prince isn't much of a decorator," he tells me. Roco smirks at that.

When I finally discover the library, I feel as if I've found the heart of the castle. Roco and Marco stand outside the door, apparently confident that nothing will harm me within the sacred walls of so many books. I've always loved libraries, always loved being surrounded by books, so many books I could never read them in a lifetime.

And this library, with its ancient scrolls and leather-bound books, is full of its own kind of magic. The room has a high ceiling spanning several floors, with stairs going up, and tall rolling ladders spread throughout to help access books and scrolls on the highest shelves. It smells of old leather and parchment and magic and mystery. I run my hands over the spines of books I've never seen, never even heard of. Books not written or available in my world. The thought boggles my mind.

"May I help you?" a deep voice asks.

I spin around, my heart pounding. "I'm sorry, I thought I was alone."

Before me stands a tall, lithe man with long white hair and a long white beard. He wears white robes with symbols embroidered into them in silver thread. His face is unlined, though his eyes and hair give the impression of agelessness. And his ears are pointed. He looks different than the Shade. Less vampire and all Fae.

"You are never alone in here," he says. "This is my domain."

I hold out my hand. "I'm Arianna Spero."

He looks at my hand, but does not reach for it. Instead, he bows deeply. "It is an honor to meet you, Princess. I am Kal'Hallen, the Keeper of the Castle, at your service. You may call me Kal. Or Keeper."

"What does a Keeper do?" I ask.

He frowns at my question. "Why, he Keeps, of course."

Right. Obviously.

"I'm looking for information about the slave contracts in this realm. And anything I can find about how the slave trade works in this kingdom."

He nods and begins to walk down aisles while I follow. Balls of white light illuminate the large room. I point to one. "I've seen these everywhere. They are powered by magic?"

"Yes," he says.

"By you?" I guess.

His eyes widen. "How did you know?"

I shrug. "You look like the castle wizard."

His face pinches in distaste. "No. I am the Keeper of the Castle. Not a..." He flicks his wrist as if trying to get dog shit off his fingers..."wizard."

"But you are magic? You are Fae?"

He nods. "I am."

"Does that mean you too are a slave?"

He purses his lips. "There are no free Fae save for the Shade, and to call them free would be to play with the truth. All Fae are slaves to one degree or another in this world."

"And yet you are in a position of authority here?" He wears that authority in every step he takes.

"I am. Prince Fenris has bestowed upon me a great honor." We stop in front of a set of shelves lined with scrolls. "Now, what kind of information do you require, Princess?"

I tell him what I'm up to and he frowns again, but helps me. We spend the afternoon looking through books and scrolls and talking about the slave force in

Inferna and how it's been exploited. "Why can't I just make it so Kara and Julian are paid?"

"Where would the money come from?" he asks.

"I don't know. Where does any of the money come from?"

"Each realm has its specialty. For Stonehill it is lumber and defense. For the Prince of Gluttony's realm it is food and herbs. There are also taxes on the cities and villages."

"So can't they be paid from those?"

He shakes his head. "The majority of our labor force are enslaved Fae. If we had to pay them all, there would not be enough funds to survive."

I shake my head. "There is a way. It might mean a disruption in the economic functioning of this kingdom for a time, but it is possible." I think of my own world, of how it must have been for the South to transition from slave labor to paid labor.

"You are talking about war, Princess. A disruption like that would lead to war, death, and the collapse of our government."

I sigh, frustrated, and close the book I have in front of me. "If I can't fix it for everyone, can I at least pay my own girls?"

Kal shrugs. "It would be up to you to find the funds. You are unlikely to pry it from the Prince. He keeps a firm hold on finances, particularly as winter nears."

"Why do the Fae not rebel? You speak of them as if they are not your people? But don't all Fae have magic?"

He leans in to whisper, as if to even speak of such things is treasonous. "Magic is strictly forbidden unless commissioned by a Prince directly, and even then only under supervision. Even I, Keeper of the Castle, cannot perform magic without Prince Fenris giving me a direct order to do so. Under penalty of death."

"But the only way that kind of rule works is if..."

Kal nods his head, and I frown.

The only way that kind of rule works is if the Fae have been put to death for using magic so often, they gave up trying.

It's late in the afternoon, and I need to stretch and get something to eat. I thank Kal for his help and promise I'll be back the next day for more research, then I head down to the kitchen to find a snack before I seek out Kayla.

I find her in her forge, working over the blazing fire while shaping a sword. I wait, watching, until she notices me and puts her work down.

She pulls off thick gloves and smiles to me. "Arianna! I hoped you'd come by."

"I wanted to see your work." It's not a small workspace, but it feels cramped with so much equipment, and hot with the fire blazing. Hanging from a wall and sitting on tables are swords, daggers, lances, arrowheads and armor and shields.

She walks over to me. "It's not much, but it'll do. I'm in the process of fulfilling Fen's sword order. The first step is turning iron into steel through carburization."

"Carburization?"

She holds up a large hammer and iron tongs. "I add a small amount of carbon through heat and hammering. Iron is malleable and ductile and can be easily welded and forged at high temperatures. Steel, though, is very tough and, once tempered, very hard and elastic. Perfect for making weapons."

I nod, taking it all in. "I have a favor to ask you," I say. My palms are sweaty and I'm not sure if it's nerves or the heat from the forge.

"What's that?" she asks.

"I'd like you to train me. I'd like to work for you." If the only way I could pay my servants is from my own funds, then I need a job.

She laughs, then stops when she realizes I'm serious. "Oh. Well, I already have an apprentice." As if being summoned by his title, a wiry boy of no more than eleven runs in, out of breath and full of news.

"Mistress Kayla! You'll never guess what I heard at Stonehill Inn." The apprentice has green hair the color of spring grass, with matching eyes and long, pointy ears. I can't tell if he's full Fae or a Shade, but my guess is a

Shade. He's scrawny, and I'm trying to imagine him lifting the equipment required to work with metal the way Kayla does, but it's a hard mental image to latch onto.

"Daison, you know I don't like you hanging around there. It's not good for one your age."

He rolls his eyes in such typical kid fashion I can't help but grin. "I'm old enough," he says, puffing out his chest. "Besides, how do you think I'm getting you all the rich customers?"

Kayla laughs. "I'm pretty sure my reputation has a little something to do with it. But do tell, what is this amazing news I'm not going to believe?"

"The new Princess they brought in is going to be on display for the Princes, and some of the lads in town want to try to crash so they can get a better look at her. She'll be all dressed up fancy-like."

I'm assuming I'm the Princess in question, but this is news to me. Kayla looks surprised too, and glances at me with a frown. "Do you know what he's talking about?"

I shrug. "Not a clue."

Kayla looks back at her apprentice. "Daison, I'd like you to meet Princess Arianna, guest of Prince Fenris. Princess, this is my speaks-before-thinking apprentice, Daison."

I bite my lip to stop a laugh as his jaw drops open in shock. He lowers his head and bows. "I'm sorry, Your Highness. I didn't realize."

I put a hand on his shoulder. "Call me Ari. And don't worry about it. It was an honest mistake."

His pale face turns bright red and he mumbles some excuse about picking up more iron, then darts out of the smithy so fast I barely see him run.

Kayla sighs. "He's a good lad, but so very young. It's hard to remember being that age."

"I'm confused about something," I say. "I don't see any old people here, though some, like the Keeper, look old, until you look at their face. And there are children. I've seen them around the city."

"Vampires can't breed with full vampires," she explains. "They need Shades or Fae, or even humans, to breed. And once those children grow to full adult-hood, they essentially stop aging physically. For the Fae, the older we get, the whiter our hair becomes. Fae with white hair are deeply respected as elders. It takes several hundreds of years or longer to achieve their look."

So would I be considered a full vampire after I take the Blood Oath, I wondered? If so, how does that work with giving one of the princes an heir?

I want to ask more questions, but Kayla walks back to her forge and uses tongs to pick up a chunk of metal and heat it over the fire. She uses the mallet to bang on the steel, molding it into a sword. "So why do you want to work for me?"

"I need a purpose here beyond just being the princess who must choose the next king," I explain. "I've always worked hard. And...I want to be able to make my own sword, when the time comes."

She eyes me skeptically. "This isn't easy work. It requires physical strength, attention to detail and patience."

"All I'm asking for is a chance."

"You don't start out making swords. You start out sweeping," she says, holding a broom out to me.

I take it and begin sweeping.

...

Days pass. I spend early mornings training with Fen in sword, hand-to-hand combat and anything else I can get him to teach me. I spend the day working at the forge with Kayla and Daison. The boy seems thrilled to have an adult to boss around, and delights in his new raised status even as he blushes and becomes unbalanced each time I walk into the room. There, I spend my time sweeping, putting away tools, cleaning rust off devices and putting them away, cleaning the forge, hauling stock, fuel and water, whatever I'm told to do. It's back-breaking work, and by the end of the day I am exhausted, but I still manage to spend most evenings in the library with Kal, learning what I can about the history of the world in which I now live.

Each night during dinner I pepper Fen with questions, which he always answers with increasing worry in his eyes.

My body is growing stronger. I am getting more experienced with the fighting techniques Fen has been training me in, and I am actually starting to enjoy my life in Stonehill.

I'd nearly forgotten about the odd bit of information Daison first brought to us about me being put on display for the princes until Fen brings it up over dinner.

"You will need a dress," he says. "Perhaps Asher can help with this."

I laugh. "No, I can manage. I'll talk to Kayla about it tomorrow. But what do I need it for?"

He shifts uncomfortably in his seat, his eyes glancing away from me. "I have been informed you are to be presented to the princes in half a fortnight, so they can all meet you. It seems some have been grumbling that they have not had a chance to set eyes on you and this gives them a disadvantage in your selection."

The real disadvantage is how fast I'm falling for the man in front of me, but I say nothing. I can tell he's trying to keep his distance from me, even as he keeps me safe and trains me.

"Is it a formal?"

He nods.

"And will you be escorting me?"

"I suppose, yes. Though once you are there, I will be at the same level as them. That is to say, you will be no one's date, to maintain balance."

"Who decided this?"

"The Council," is all he'll say, as he stands to go. "I trust I will see you at sunup for your training?"

I nod, and he turns to leave.

That night as Kal and I pour over books, I ask him about the Council.

"The Council consists of the seven princes. They were meant to be advisors to the king. When a matter was in dispute, the king had the princes vote on a matter and usually abided by the majority rule."

I tell Kal what they have commanded of me, and he frowns. "I have never heard of this. It is not a custom or tradition that has been done before."

"I guess there's a lot involving me that's new."

"That would be quite true," he says.

"Why do you think the king wanted me here so badly?" I ask.

"I have given that considerable thought," he says, his hands idling over one of his beloved books. "But I do not have an answer. It is completely unorthodox, even for a king who changed much of his policies toward the end of his life."

"Kal, I have a question..."

"How shocking," he says totally deadpan.

I laugh. "I know, I'm usually so timid and reserved."

That gets a guffaw out of him.

"But seriously, I'm curious. How would some-one from my world contact a demon to make a deal? Somehow my mother managed to do this, but I can't for the life of me figure out how."

He lifts my right hand and flips it over, revealing the symbol on my wrist. "That is a demon mark. It is unique to each demon. Yours is the sign of Lucian, who originally made the deal with your mother. When you agreed to their contract, you became part of that deal and thus took his mark. Your mother would have had to know his mark and draw it in blood to summon him."

"So as long as you have blood, you can summon any demon if you know their mark?"

Kal nods. "Indeed, that is the way of it."

"Do Fae have these too?"

"No, we do not. We use a much older magic, some would say. At any rate, it is very different."

...

I tell Kayla of my need for a formal dress the next day and she agrees to help me shop for the materials required to have it made.

My time in the forge, though hard, sweaty, dirty work, has been rewarding thus far. I learn a lot just by watching her shape and sharpen steel into all manner of weapons. What surprises me is how much time she also spends crafting regular everyday items, like nails and doors and locks. But I think some of my favorite work of hers is her jewelry. Her designs are magical, and she uses crystals found throughout the city to make them more amazing.

"Would you teach me how to do this too someday? When I'm ready?" I ask, holding up a ring.

She nods. "When you're ready."

Daison trips into the smithy, all knees and elbows and blushes. He stutters when he says hi to me, and I smile and try to make him more comfortable. He can't make eye contact with me, but he's holding something small wrapped in leather that he shoves into my hands. "I heard it was recently your birthday, so I made you this."

My birthday. That seems like forever ago, but it was really just a few weeks. I take his gift and let the leather fall open to reveal a small dagger stuck into a custom black leather scabbard with silver designs. I pull it out and admire the edge, sharpened to a deadly degree. The blade has graceful leaves carved into the steel. "This is beautiful," I say, honestly. "I will cherish it."

He grins, looking up at me long enough to see that my words are genuine. On impulse, I reach over and hug him. He staggers in my arms, then wraps his around me and returns the hug, before pulling away.

When he runs out, I strap the dagger around my waist and admire the way it hangs at my hip. "He does good work," I say.

Kayla grins. "He did learn from the best. But I'm surprised he gave that to you. He's been working on it for a year."

I look at her, stunned. "A year? I can't accept this," I say, reaching to take it off.

She places a hand on mine to stop me. "You must. It would break his heart if you refused. He's quite taken with you. I think you remind him of his mother."

"What's she like?" I ask, realizing I know very little about him.

"She was beautiful, like you," she says. "Fae, of course. A slave. She was raped by a vampire and left for dead, pregnant with him. She died when he was a young child, though no one knows how. I suspect the vampire who attacked her came back to finish the job. He would have gone after the child too, but Daison was smart, clever. He hid until it was safe. I found him days later, his dead mother still in their home. That's when I took him in as my apprentice. I made up a story about him to cast off suspicion. He's a Shade, so he couldn't be enslaved, but it wouldn't have gone well for him if he'd been left to fend for himself, either."

My throat tightens at the story, and I fight a wave of sadness imagining what that poor boy has been through. "Did anyone catch the vampire who hurt his mother?"

Kayla laughs a bitter laugh. "No one ever looked for him. She was a slave. Property. Nothing."

I feel sick, struggling to think of what to say when we hear a scream from outside. Kayla and I run around the back of the forge, where Kayla keeps a wagon she loads up with weapons to deliver to Fen, or other customers as needed. Daison was meant to transfer the new supply of swords to the wagon, but something is wrong.

Another scream comes from behind the wagon, which looks off-centered, as if it's been knocked to the side.

Kayla and I rush around the wagon. Daison is trapped under a broken wheel, his body contorted in such a way that he doesn't even look human. His leg bent backwards at the knee. He is so pale, and his blood is seeping into the ground. Kayla screams at me, and I move to help lift the wagon off him, but it's full of steel swords, and I'm only human. Not strong enough to lift this. I bend down next to Daison, who is slipping in and out of consciousness. I brush the hair off his sweaty brow, my eyes flooding with tears. "You're okay, kid. We're going to get you out of this. Just hold my hand."

His hand, so cold and still, does not move in mine, and I fear we've already lost him.

Kayla curses under breath, as if arguing with herself about something. She seems to come to some kind of decision and bends down next to Daison, pulling out a pendant I've never seen before, tucked under her tunic. She holds the stone in her hand and mumbles words in a language I've never heard, but somehow feels familiar, like something from a dream I once had.

As she speaks, the wagon begins to lift off Daison, who is so still in my arms. I pull him out before the wagon falls, then watch in amazement as Kayla leans over him and rests her stone on his chest as she continues to chant.

A thick piece of wood sticks out of his abdomen. She pulls it out and straightens his twisted leg. He screams so loud I have to resist covering my ears.

But as Kayla continues to chant, his body begins to mend, and his breathing levels out. Color returns to his face.

"We must get him back to my house," she says, lifting the boy's body easily in her arms. I follow them as she moves quickly through the streets and into a cottage near a waterfall surrounded by trees and the mountains. It's more remote than the other houses. I follow them in, and she guides me to a small bedroom to the right where Daison usually sleeps. I turn down his bed and she lays him in it, then covers him up and says one more chant before ushering me out of the room.

Her cottage is small. She sleeps upstairs in a small room. Daison sleeps down here. There's a hearth with a fireplace and a pot hanging over it, a small kitchen packed with herbs and fresh food, and a living room with a few comfortable chairs and cushions on the floor. Kayla makes us both some tea and sits down in the chair next to me as we both stare at the fire.

"That was magic," I say.

She nods, sipping her tea. "And if you tell anyone what you saw, Daison and I will be executed."

"Fen would never do that!" I say, hoping I'm right.

"He would have no choice. And it doesn't matter. If he didn't, someone else would. It is the way things are. My life, Arianna, is now in your hands." She looks over to Daison's bedroom door. "His life is now in your hands."

10

SLAVE TO THE PAST

"I am the Prince of War. I do not 'lighten up'."
—Fenris Vane

Daison makes a remarkable recovery, and though it takes a few days, Kayla stops eyeing me with a worried frown, as if I might shout her secret from the rooftops at any moment.

I'm not telling anyone.

Not even Fen.

When he asks about our dress shopping that night, I admit we didn't get around to it.

"She got busy at the forge," I say. "All those swords you need. For that war you won't tell me about."

He huffs at that. "We just need to be prepared for all eventualities."

The distance between us is growing, and I'm not sure what to do about it. We have breakfast and dinner together every day. We train every morning. But there's a wall between us, one he keeps adding to each time he turns away from my gaze, or pulls away from my touch.

"I will call Asher. He can help you with your gown. That man spends far too much time watching fashion reality television when we are in your world. It's not natural."

I nearly choke on the apple I'm eating. "I'm just trying to picture him glued to your big screen screaming at the television when the wrong person wins," I say, smiling.

"That's about the whole of it," Fen says seriously.

"And to think, he acted like he'd never heard of reality television when we first met," I say, thinking back to the day I found out about all of this.

Fen smirks. "He is quite attached. It is his secret shame, I think. If he were not a prince of hell and vampire condemned to the darkness of your world, I do believe he would make a career of it."

"He does have good taste," I say. "If you like that kind of thing," I add, when Fen raises an eyebrow at me. "Your leather and cotton look has its own kind of charm. More Viking than GQ, but there's a market for that," I assure him.

I almost see a flicker of a smile on his lips before we are interrupted by a soldier who requires Fen's attention on the training field.

Fen excuses himself and Baron stays with me as I finish my dinner in silence.

The next day, Asher shows up with an entourage carrying silks and satins in all shades. "Darling, I have been informed you are in crisis mode and are in need of a dress. I am here to save you."

I smile at the absurdity of him, but I let him direct the circus of people he's brought. Under his direction, red and white material is chosen, and Asher instructs his servants on how to design the gown in such a way as to flaunt my best features. They take measurements of every inch of my body, then rush out with orders to make haste sewing.

When I ask Asher about this presenting I'll be attending, he shrugs. "I, unfortunately, was called away on business when the Council met about this. We will both be surprised, no dout. I'm guessing formal cocktail hour at High Castle, with you as the guest of honor. You'll be dashing, I assure you."

I'm still nervous about the whole ordeal, but how bad could it be? I've found my footing here, and I do want to meet the rest of the princes. I walk Asher out of the castle and through Stonehill, enjoying a few minutes without work.

"You look well," he acknowledges as we approach the gate. "This life is agreeing with you."

"Thank you," I say. "I'm finding ways of staying busy."

He smiles, and his attractiveness is not lost on me, but neither does it make my knees shake. I know who I have to blame for that, thank you very much.

"I've heard the people speaking of you in hushed admiration," he says. "They like you. A lot. The vampires, the Shade, even the slaves. I don't think any of us were expecting that."

I cock my head. "Did you expect I would be horrible and hated?"

He grins. "Not exactly. We just didn't realize you would have everyone falling in love with you so quickly."

"Surely not everyone," I say, thinking of Fen and the way he pulls his hands away from me when he finds them lingering too long during our training.

Asher winks at me before walking away. "You might be surprised, Princess."

...

That day Kayla steals me away from the forge and we travel through Stonehill on a quest. Well, at least I call it a quest. Kayla rolls her eyes. "You'll need proper jewelry for this little party the princes are planning. Daison is manning my booth at the moment. We'll find you something perfect to match your gown."

Stonehill is deceptively large. At first glance, because of the mountains surrounding it, perhaps, it seems quaint. Charming. And it is, but it's more expansive than I realized. The very wealthy and well-connected vampire lords live in large manors built into the mountains, their roofs often displaying elaborate gardens and sculptures. Most of the Shade live in small clusters of modest thatch housing spotted with flower beds and potted plants. Each district has its own name and personality, though I am still trying to remember them all. There is Centerhill, the commerce district, full of shops and street-side booths. So far, it's the most flavorful and exciting. It's where Kayla leads me now.

Her booth is well-positioned near the city center. Trees sway in the wind and the land smells sweet from an overnight rainfall that left everything with a watery sheen under the struggling sun. We walk to Kayla's booth and Daison smiles at us, his cheeks turning red. I do hope one day he will feel more comfortable with me.

"Daison, bring out my best jewelry. Particularly the rubies. We need something special for Ari."

Daison nods and pulls out a small box tied in soft suede. Kayla opens it and exposes white, yellow and rose gold necklaces with different precious stones designed into them. I try on a ruby and diamond necklace that would work well with the fabric and style of dress Asher chose for me. "What do you think—"

"Slave sale! Slave sale!" Two Shade children run past yelling.

Kayla frowns, and we both turn to the city center. It's surrounded by trees with a platform in the middle for public presentations and performances and benches for sitting. Already a large crowd has gathered, and on the stage stand five Fae shackled to each other. They are all women who look young and scared. Except for the middle girl. She doesn't look mad, she looks pissed and ready to spit in the face of anyone who comes close. She's got bruises and scratch marks all over her pale body. My guess is she's already put up a fight at least once.

A tall man dressed in fine red fabrics and meticulously styled stands on the stage. He is a vampire and commanding in his presence. There are guards everywhere, but I don't recognize any of them from Fen's people. They don't wear Fen's colors either.

"Who are the guards?" I ask.

"They belong to a wealthy family in the Time Pool district."

The man begins to speak, and the crowd quiets to listen. "My brother, Lord Tylin, recently died in our constant war against the rebels of the Outlands, the Fae anomalies who would try to claim our world. He leaves behind these five slaves, captured as spoils of war."

Kayla shakes her head. "His brother didn't die in war. He died in a bar fight against a Shade. That Shade was hanged quietly and without a trial even though Tylin initiated the fight. This whole thing is a farce."

"Can't Fen do something?" I ask.

"Fen is a good man, but he is myopic in his focus. He has no idea what's going on in his realm. His sole focus is war."

The bidding begins, and many wealthy looking men and women raise the bid. There is one man, a vampire in the back with white hair and cold eyes, who keeps upping the bid. He makes my skin crawl, though he hasn't noticed me. I have no idea what my plan is, or why I do what I do, but I step forward and offer the highest bid I can think of for the girls.

Kayla stares at me, shocked. Everyone in the crowd looks at me. I want to retreat and hide, but I've made my stance and I can't back down now. "I wish to buy all five girls," I declare to everyone.

The soldiers prowling the crowds walk over to me, menacingly. Kayla pulls her sword out and holds it at her side. I wish I had a sword, but I console myself with the dagger I have at my hip.

Baron bares his teeth at the guards and Kayla pushes herself close to one of them, raising her blade. "Do you dare threaten your future Queen?"

The man at the podium whistles, and they all stand down.

"Why is everyone acting so strange?" I whisper to Kayla.

"Because that man with the white hair is a prince of hell, and you just challenged him," she says quietly.

"Likely he had a deal already made with Tylin's brother to buy the slaves at a discount in exchange for a favor."

I look at the man again, and this time he does notice me. His face is hard, and I get the impression he would attack me on the spot if not for everyone around us.

"Which prince is he?"

"Levi, Prince of Envy," she says. "Be careful of him."

Levi outbids me, and I counter. I've been studying Fen's financials and his realm's affairs for a few weeks now, and I feel like I have a good handle on what he can afford. We've got this. I hope.

Levi finally stops bidding, and I am declared the new owner of the girls. I command my own guards, Marco and Roco, to escort the girls back to the castle safely, and to arrange for Kara and Julian to care for them. Marco argues with me, but I insist I'll be fine without him, and Kayla promises she and Baron will keep me safe, so he finally, reluctantly agrees.

The crowd disperses and I take a deep breath, adrenaline still pulsing through me. "Does that happen often?"

"When there are new prisoners of war taken, which happens fairly often, or when someone of nobility dies, which happens much less often," she says. "Vampires aren't easy to kill, but it is possible. Fae aren't too easy to kill either, for that matter."

"And Shade?" I ask.

"In some ways, we're the hardest to kill of all." She winks at me and I smile, but it fades quickly when I think about what we just witnessed.

"How can you stand it, seeing your own people auctioned off like cattle?" I don't mean for my question to sound judgmental, but she snaps back anyway.

"They aren't my people. The Fae hate Shades. They would kill all vampires, half my blood family, if they could. My mother was Fae, yes. She spent her days washing floors on her knees and her nights with men she despised. She never fought for herself. For her family. She was weak. I can't be weak. I don't fit into either world, but at least here, with Fen, I am accepted and given a place of respect. That wouldn't be true in the Outlands, or anywhere else. So I take what I can, and I do my best to live my life with some manner of peace."

I don't know what to say, so I say nothing. Instead, I lay my hand on hers and squeeze. It's a silent show of support. A way to say that even though I am confused and conflicted about the rules of this world, I still care about her and accept her as she is. It's the best I can do, but it seems to be enough.

We return to the booth, and I select a ruby necklace lined with silver and diamonds. Then we head back to the forge, and as the day progresses, I notice a subtle shift in my relationship with Kayla. I'm no longer assigned to sweeping floors and putting away tools. It's as if I've somehow proven myself to her.

She finally begins to teach me the craft of blacksmithing. "You'll start with your first sword," she says. "I'll help you make it, from beginning to end. It's the only way to learn."

And so we start with iron, and turn it into steel. And the process begins. A true alchemy. Like the iron, I am becoming something new. Something I don't quite understand.

I have felt it for a few weeks now, but haven't had the words to articulate it. There's something in me pushing to be free. A raw power, trapped by training, by my world, by my past. But I am growing. I am shaping my body and mind just as surely as I'm shaping my sword from steel. Soon, I will become something new.

...

That night over dinner, Fen waits for me to broach the subject of the slaves I acquired. "I assume you've heard," I say, sipping my drink and watching his body language across the table.

He stares at his dinner as he talks. "Indeed. I think all the realms have heard at this point."

"I take it Levi isn't happy?"

Fen snorts. "Levi is never happy. It's a byproduct of his curse. I do think envy is the worst of all the seven sins. To never be content with what you have. To always covet what others possess. Miserable way to live."

"Are you angry?"

Finally, he looks up at me, his piercing blue eyes holding mine. "Should I be?"

I shrug. "I have no idea. You don't share much these days."

"I am not mad, Arianna. I admire what you're trying to do. But you must know, you can't save them all. That's not the way this world works. There's more to our history than you understand."

I bristle at that. "I've been doing my research. Kal has been helping me understand."

He shakes his head. "You can research the history of this world, but you can't know what I lived through. You can't know through words what I have learned through blood."

I exhale at that, my body slumping in my chair. "I have to try, Fen. I have to at least try to help the people who need it."

For the first time in weeks he reaches his hand out to mine and holds it in his. The warmth and strength of him pulses through me, and my fingers run over the raised demon mark on his wrist, memorizing the curves and patterns. His curse. His duty.

A heavy silence fills the space between us, connects us together in a palpable way. I breathe him in, feel his pulse, revel in all the unspoken words between us. There's so much I want to say. So much I want him to understand, and so much I want to know.

I'm about to try, about to open my mouth, and my heart, and tell him what I'm feeling, when a young man bursts in to the dining area. He bows, then hands Fen a parchment sealed in wax. "I was told to deliver this to you immediately, Your Highness."

"Thank you," I tell the messenger. "Ask our cook to get you something to eat and drink before you head out."

He bows to me, mumbles a thank you and leaves us.

Fen reads the letter quickly, frowning deeply. When he's done, he stands abruptly and curses.

"What's wrong?" I ask, standing as well. Baron leaps to his feet with us, ears perked, teeth bared, ready to fight whatever is making his master angry.

"You must have really pissed Levi off. He's insisting I bring you to High Castle tonight to meet the princes."

"But that wasn't supposed to happen for another week. I don't even have my dress yet."

"Asher had it delivered this afternoon. It's in your room."

"It's so late," I argue. This doesn't feel right, but I'm not sure why.

"We have to go. The Council decided it."

"Why are you never there when they decide things about me?" I ask.

"Because I'm never informed until after the fact." He practically growls, and I can tell his temper is tethered by a string.

"Doesn't that seem fishy to you?"

"It does. But you will be safe. Levi wouldn't dare make a play at you with everyone there."

I nod. "I'll go get ready."

...

I bathe in the waterfall shower, then Kara and Julian brush out and dry my hair and help me dress. I wear the necklace Kayla loaned me, and when I look in the mirror, I have to admit I look like a princess. I smile. "Thank you, ladies."

They both curtsy.

I turn to them. "I haven't had a chance to talk to you about the slaves I bought today. I want them treated well. Please make sure they have comfortable jobs they enjoy and are under the care of people you trust."

Julian nods. "We will."

"I'll check in on them when all this is done."

As a last measure, I strap my dagger to my inner thigh. Just in case.

I meet Fen downstairs, at the entrance of the castle. He's dressed nicer than I've ever seen him, in a black vest with gold buttons and a red shirt beneath. "Did you borrow that from Asher?" I ask with a teasing smile.

He narrows his eyes at me. "No. I do know how to dress appropriately for an occasion."

"You look good," I say. "But I prefer you in leather."

I wink at him and straighten the lapel of his coat. Our bodies are close. This time, we're not holding swords; he's not teaching me to kill someone. This time it's just us, so I press closer. He holds my hand, pressing it tight against his chest.

"I have something for you," he says.

I step back as he pulls out a small leather pouch from his pocket and hands it to me. "I commissioned Kayla to make it."

When I open the pouch, tears burn my eyes. Inside, lies a white gold ring with a Shooting Star Crystal in the center and beautiful root designs on the sides. I slip it on my middle finger and admire it. "Thank you," I whisper.

"You're welcome." He holds out his arm, and I slide mine into his as we walk through Stonehill to the boat that will take us to High Castle.

I know this is hard for him. Hard for us both. Why grow closer to someone who will leave you in less than a month?

But this ring is a reminder. There is something between us. And no matter what happens, I will always be grateful for Fenris Vane.

...

When we arrive, trailed by Marco and Roco, we are greeted by six armed guards. They escort us to the ballroom, where the floors glitter with gold and paintings of war cover the arching ceiling. More guards, clad in red and black armor, line the walls and doors.

"Whose men are these?" I ask Fen, clinging to his arm.

"Levi's," he says with a growl.

The ballroom is empty save for us and the guards. A raised platform carved from marble stands in the middle. One of the guards grabs my arm. "The princess must—"

Fen grabs the man's wrist, twisting it until the guard collapses to his knees. "You will not touch her," growls the prince.

"Of course. Apologies, Your Highness." He glances between Fen and me as he speaks, clearly unsure about which of us he should apologize to first. After a moment, Fen releases his grip.

The guard stands, cradling his limp wrist. "The princess must situate herself in the center." He points to the platform with his good arm.

Fen is about to argue, but I place a hand on him. "I'll be fine. Let's just get this over with."

I walk to the platform. Fen keeps Baron by his side. Once I'm 'situated', the floating lights in the ballroom flicker off, and we are left in complete darkness. A bright yellow sphere begins to glow ahead, blinding me. It's a spotlight, and I am the focus. I hear others enter the room, presumably the other princes, but I can't see them.

"What's this about, Levi?" Fen demands.

"It's just our way of getting to know the princess." His voice is cold and smooth like polished stone. "You've had her all to yourself long enough."

"Everyone will have their time with the princess," Asher says offhandedly. "No need to worry yourself."

"Says the man who has already met her," another voice says.

"Oh, Niam, has our brother here pulled you into another one of his sad conspiracy theories?" Asher asks. "You know Levi is always bitter, but you shouldn't let him get to you too."

"We just thought it best we all have a chance to talk to the princess," Niam says.

"She is quite the prize," another voice says. I recognize him from just one meeting. Dean, Prince of Lust. This time, my knees don't go weak.

"It seems curious that so many of us weren't invited to the recent Council meeting where so many of these decisions were made," says Asher, who seems the most level-headed right now. I'm pretty sure if Fen tried to talk, he'd just start fighting.

"What can we say," Levi says. "You've been awfully preoccupied with other endeavors of late, Asher. Where have you been disappearing to so often?"

"Some of us have real work to do," Asher says. "We can't just sit around all day wishing we had what our brothers have."

There's a thud. Then a groan, and then Asher laughs. I suspect Levi must have punched him. "Now, now, brothers," says a new voice. "We're here. The princess is here. Let's just get on with it, shall we? I have work to do and no time for this rot."

"Shut it, Ace," Levi spits. "You aren't in charge here."

Ace laughs. "Nor are you, dear Levi. And that rankles you, doesn't it?"

"What is the plan for our girl, here?" Asher asks.

Levi answers. "We have some questions for her first."

"Let's have at it then," Asher says. "What are your questions?"

I suck in my breath and exhale slowly, trying to calm my nerves. My legs shake and there's nowhere to sit. Whoever came up with this idea just lost their chance at the crown.

"What criteria will you take into consideration when choosing your mate?" Levi asks.

Just his voice makes me want to punch something. "For one thing, I'll consider if the prince in question is a complete ass who would treat a woman like an animal in a circus. Spoiler alert, that will not impress."

Fen barks a quick laugh and I smirk a little, knowing he'll see it.

I hear Niam's voice next. "So you have already developed opinions about princes you haven't met?"

"My opinions come from my direct experience of you. For some, that bodes well. For others, let's just say you're definitely making an impression, just not a favorable one."

The lights are hot and my throat is getting dry. A rivulet of sweat drips down my spine, making my skin itch. Someone clears their throat to ask another question, but I interrupt. "What is this about? Why are you guys behaving like spoiled toddlers fighting over a toy? Do you really think this will impress me? It's my understanding that—"

"You don't speak to a prince like that!" Levi roars.

"And you don't speak to the princess and future Queen like that," Fen says in his deep, gravelly voice.

"I thought you didn't want to be involved," Niam says. "Seems like you're pretty invested in it now."

"Enough!" Levi says. "It's clear we won't get more answers from her. It's time for the revealing."

I stiffen. His voice sounds lecherous and my stomach rolls. Dean smirks. "Sounds delightful."

Levi continues. "Princess, you are to undress and present yourself to us for examination. If you resist, the guards will be forced to finish the job."

"You bastard!" I scream.

Someone snaps. "Guards!" Four armored men approach me. I kick one in the knee. He stumbles back. Someone grabs me from behind. Hands pull at my dress. They tear away at my clothes.

Baron growls. He jumps into the light, knocking one of the men to the ground.

Tears burn my eyes. Not from sadness. From rage.

I grab the dagger from my inner thigh.

And stab a guard in the arm.

His grip loosens. But there are still two pairs of hands on me. They rip off what remains of my top. I slash at them, screaming and spitting. One of them grabs my wrist. He is strong. Too strong. My fingers ache. I drop the dagger.

And then he is there. Fen.

He grabs a guard by the throat and squeezes. The man's neck explodes with bits of blood and meat and bone. The other man stumbles back, pleading for his life. It is too late.

They have unleashed the Prince of War.

Fen leaps into the air. His knee slams into the man's head and sends him to the floor. The man groans in pain, his face a mangled mess of purple and red. His nose is caved in. Still, I recognize him. The guard who grabbed me earlier. Fen stands above him. "I told you not to touch her."

He slams his foot down into the man's face.

It shatters.

All goes silent. Red stains the marble platform. Bits of bone litter the floor.

Fen faces the light where the remaining princes sit. His hair is dark with blood, and he roars an inhuman war cry. "Does anyone else challenge me?"

Someone claps. "Impressive dear brother," says Levi. "No challenge. I will have my time with the princess." I see a shadow move in the darkness. It disappears through a door. Others follow.

Fen passes me what remains of my torn top, stained with crimson, and I cover my chest with the rags.

Asher steps into the light. "This is a fine mess we've gotten ourselves into," he says, looking down at a splash of blood that touched his sleeve.

Fen reaches for me, ignoring his brother. "Are you hurt?"

I'm shaking, and it's hard to talk. "I don't know. Not badly, I don't think."

He embraces me, pulls me tight against his body. I can feel his heart beat frantically beneath his clothing. His muscles are tense and flexed under my hands. He is still ready for battle, but I can tell he's trying to calm himself.

When he steps away from me to address the brothers who remain, I realize I'm no longer shaking.

"I need to get her home." He turns to Asher. "You need to find out what Levi is thinking."

"It seems you've got the better end of this deal," Asher says. But he doesn't argue as Fen takes my hand and escorts me out.

...

Kara and Julian don't speak as they help me bathe and rub ointment into my bruises. When I'm in my night-gown I cross the hall to Fen's room and let myself in. He paces the room, bathed as well and dressed in fresh clothing.

When he sees me he crosses the room and wraps his arms around me. I fall into his touch. We speak no words. He carries me to bed and there, in the silence of night, he holds me. He holds me as I curse at the past and groan at the pain.

He holds me as I cry.

11

DIGGING UP LIES

"Ace is brilliant. He's also lazy, or so he says."
—Fenris Vane

"I think it's time for you to visit your friends back home," Fen says during breakfast.

When I woke this morning, he had already left to hunt with Baron. I was half way through my meal when they joined me.

I feel a pang of shame at his words. It's been too long since I even thought of home, so immersed have I been in this new life. But the thought of seeing Es and Pete again raises my spirits and makes the aches and pains I have from being beat up last night more bearable. And when I fantasize about proper coffee, and internet, and all the trapping of modernity that I miss, I actually smile. Then I groan because my lip is split and my jaw is bright purple from a nasty bruise.

"You should ice that," Fen says.

"I have."

"I'm sorry that happened to you," he says. "I should have known it wasn't going to end well. I will kill Levi for this."

"As much as I'd love to cheer you on in that desire, wouldn't that cause some problems? Like internal war?"

"I am the Prince of War. They will not win against me. And not all the brothers will join Levi."

I sigh. "Let's just get through the war with the Fae first. Then we can deal with your brother. But Fen…"

He raises a scarred eyebrow at me, waiting.

"I'm not spending a month with that man. I won't." I shudder at the thought, but then I think of my mother, of her soul, of the suffering she would endure. "You have to help me. You have to help me keep my mother safe."

"You have my word," he says.

My head throbs with pain, and I sip at my juice, wishing it were something stronger. "I don't suppose you have aspirin or something in this world?"

"No. But I'll have the healer mix you something for the pain. And there is always alcohol."

I nod my thanks and drain my cup, then stand. "When do we leave?"

"I have some things I must see to, but we can leave at sunset."

"Right. We can't go by day, can we?"

"Not easily," he says.

I'm so used to seeing him, all of them, out during the day here. It's easy to forget my own world isn't as hospitable.

After breakfast I head back to my quarters to take a bath and dress for the day. There's a hot cup of…something by my bed when I exit my bath, with a note from Fen. "Drink. Be well. Stay safe."

I sip it, wrinkle my nose, then drink as fast as the hot liquid will allow. It's vile, but it makes me feel better almost instantly. "Bless you, Fen," I whisper as my headache and body aches disappear. I might be imagining it, but even my bruises and cuts seem to be healing faster. This is way better than Tylenol!

I walk to the forge, and Kayla helps me with my sword. We spend the entire day on it, making good progress. I should have my very first blade soon. She asks about what happened last night, and I give her the grim details.

She hugs me. "Levi will pay for this," she says. "I swear it."

I laugh, but inside I'm shaking. I fear my new friends will risk their lives and the lives of their people against another prince of hell. But I'm not sure what the answer is, because Levi is a threat to me. I cannot be left in his care. I'm not sure I would make it out alive.

...

My excitement at going home is growing, and when I return to the castle, I'm ready. There's a knock at my bedroom door, and I open it expecting Fen, but instead it's a man I do not recognize. He's handsome, with a sculpted face, dark hair that's a bit wayward, though short enough not to be too messy, and a dark shadow of hair on his jawline.

He bows. "It's an honor to officially meet you." A giant watch-like contraption wraps around his wrist. Sturdy bags and tools hang from his belt.

"You're Ace," I say.

He smiles. "How did you—"

"I was told you're quite the inventor."

"Ah, yes." He checks his watch gizmo. "I've come to fetch you. Well, actually, I came to fetch Fen, but he insists he cannot leave without you. Apparently, last night raised his hackles. Let me assure you, I voted against the whole debacle."

"Having someone under your protection physically assaulted and sexually violated does annoy some," I say coldly.

Ace laughs. "You are as saucy as Asher said." He holds up his hands in surrender. "I'm no threat to you, Arianna. I'm here to help. Fen is finishing up something, and he asked me to look after you until we can leave."

"Where are we going?" I close the door behind me and walk with Ace down the winding staircase to the parlor. A fireplace blazes in the center, and we each take seats in front. Julian brings us both wine and a platter of cheese, bread and fruit.

Ace takes a bite of strawberry, then licks his fingers. "We are going to High Castle to dig up my father's remains."

"So the Council agreed then?" I ask, sipping at the sweet wine.

Ace smirks. "Nope, that's why it's just me and Fen. And you, apparently," he says as an afterthought. "The High Council can't know. But even Zeb agrees we must determine what killed King Lucian, for it was not the poison."

"Do you have any suspects?" I ask.

"Levi certainly hasn't done himself any favors. But we have no proof of anything yet," he says.

"Fen was going to take me home tonight," I say. "It was part of my contract, that I could go home once a month to check on my mother and friends."

Ace leans back in his chair and pops a grape in his mouth. "That will have to wait. Sorry about that. And I do feel your pain. Your world is extraordinary. I used to go there often. Not just for feeding, but to surround myself with such wonderful inventions."

"You don't go anymore?" I ask.

He shakes his head. "It's too painful."

"The sun?"

"No, the promise of things that cannot be." He looks at me, a bittersweet expression on his handsome face. "Has Fen told you much about our curse?"

"He doesn't like talking about it," I say. "I know only that you are each cursed with what we would call one of the seven deadly sins. That you are powerful and immortal, but also mortally wounded by my sun. You're vampires."

He nods. "There's more though. Have you noticed how we seem to live in a medieval time trap?"

"Really?" I ask sarcastically.

"And perhaps you also noticed that some of my brothers seem...eternally stuck in adolescent angst and lack maturity?"

I laugh darkly. "I've wondered. With so much time, so much life, how could any of you stay stuck in your miserable patterns?"

"It's part of the curse," he says. "Perhaps the worst part. We are stuck in time, trapped in all ways. We can't really grow, learn or mature past the points we are now. When I'm in your world, I can comprehend the technological innovations that led to such greatness. I know how I could replicate that here, and bring us into a new age. But the moment I step through the mirror, that knowledge disappears like mist in the sun. I grasp at it, remembering the promise of it, but I can never hold on to the details long enough to do anything about it. My inventions are crude attempts to capture even a phantom replica of what I once knew. I was driving myself mad each time I went to your world, so I stopped going."

"Has it helped? To stay here?"

"Some," he says, staring at the fire. "Some. But those dream-like memories are still there, taunting me. It is better to not know something than to know it but not remember."

Fen walks in with Baron, and we both stand.

"Has Ace explained what's to happen tonight?"

I nod. "We're digging up your father."

"Ace and I are digging. You are watching and staying close to me," Fen says. "I'm sorry about your trip home. We'll go soon, I promise."

I nod and walk with them to the boat. The nights are getting colder, and I hug my cloak around my body and watch my breath turn white as I exhale. At least it will be warmer near High Castle.

"Where's his body?" I ask as Ace guides the boat to dock near the castle.

"In a mausoleum behind the castle," Fen says.

We hike around the fortress in the dead of night with no moonlight to guide us. Princes of hell might have great eyesight in the dark, but I'm having a hard time seeing.

Baron seems to be the only one concerned about my ability to hike in the darkness, and he stands by my side to help guide me. I give him a pat on the head for his attention.

Blue light shines in the distance. As we near, I realize they are blue orbs hovering around the mausoleum. It is a giant structure of gray stone, decorated with carvings of battles and parties and a man resembling the one I had seen in a painting. Tall, broad shouldered, his face hard, his presence regal. Lucian.

Ace glances at the picture of his father. Fen does not. The door is shut, and he pulls the stone slab open, his muscles bulging under his dark leather coat.

Stale air escapes, filling my lungs with the dust of the dead. I choke on it, then take a few deep breaths of clean air before joining Ace and Fen inside.

It's a small room, lit with blue light. An ornate bust of Lucian rests on a marble pillar in the center. "Where's the coffin?" I ask, looking around.

Fen points to the bust. "Below."

Ace sighs and opens the large bag he's been carrying. He pulls out two wickedly sharp pick axes. "That's why I brought these." He tosses one to Fen who grabs if from the air effortlessly. "Get to digging, brother."

Baron and I are chased from the room by dust and the sound of marble shattering, as Ace and Fen destroy the bust and platform to get to the coffin.

I sit where Fen can see me, at his insistence, just outside the mausoleum, my back leaning against the cool stone. Baron lays his head on my lap, and we both try to ignore the noise.

It seems to take hours. Fen and Ace are both sweaty and dirty by the time they are done.

I stand and stretch, dusting plaster off my body in vain. I look down the hole they created. "How will you get it out?" I ask.

They dug a space around the casket. Both men jump into the hole and grab the lid.

"Together?" asks Ace.

"Together."

They push open the casket, and the lid clatters to the ground.

"Shit," Fen says, looking inside.

I move closer to see and then gag and pull away. "What happened to him?" His body is a blackened shriveled up lump. Nothing resembling a man remains.

"Someone has defiled his body," Ace says, frowning. "We'll never get any answers from him now."

Fen slams his fist on the side of the casket. "Whoever did this knew we were coming."

Ace's eyes go wide. "Wait. You think it was me?"

"No." Fen grabs the lid and covers the casket once again. "But it was someone on the High Council."

Realization dawns on Ace's face. "You think the vote tipped them off. They knew we'd come here even without permission. At least, they suspected."

Fen clasps his brother's shoulder. "Arianna cannot stay with each prince. It is not safe."

"But the contract...no. You're right. We'll find a way."

"What does this mean?" I ask.

"It means you are in more danger than we realized," says Fen. "Tomorrow night we'll head back to your world. In the meantime, keep your guards and Baron close. I need to have a chat with my brothers privately."

"Don't do anything stupid," I say.

He smiles, but it's a smile full of menace. "They are the ones who should be worried."

...

I spend the next day working on my sword, which is nearly done thanks to Kayla's help. And that night, Fen keeps his promise and takes me home.

It doesn't take long for the boat to arrive at the magic mirror that will whisk us back to the mansion. I'm excited to see my friends, but the worry that weighs on Fen also affects me. There are too many unknowns, too many dangers: the Fae who tried to kidnap me, a killer amongst the princes. All of it is tied to my mother's fate. Still, I try to let it all go for a few hours so I can enjoy my time in my world. "How will I explain who you are to my friends?"

"A business acquaintance?" he suggests.

"Who insists on being with me every single moment of my very personal visit to see my dying mother and visit my best friends?"

He frowns. "What do you suggest?"

"You'll have to pretend to be my boyfriend," I say.

He doesn't reply, but I know I have him.

Baron isn't happy we are leaving without him, but how could we possibly explain a giant white wolf with us? He is much too wolfy to pass as a Husky or mix. So we leave him at Stonehill and promise to be back soon. I only get half a day—or a night rather, but I'm going to make the most of it.

As we step out of the mansion and the limo pulls up to greet us, I realize I haven't had to worry about cars for a few weeks, and I actually forgot I'd need one when in Portland.

I tremble as I climb into the back. Fen sits next to me, though there were other seats, and he holds my hand. "We can overcome our fears," he says quietly, as we pull away from the mansion.

I squeeze his hand, pulling it closer to my body, enjoying the weight of his arm over my legs. I want more of this closeness, but he only offers it for comfort, not for pleasure or true intimacy.

It has the intended result. I'm no longer scared of being in a car. Perhaps everything I've gone through in hell has changed me. I breathe deeply and smile, enjoying a car ride for the first time in my life.

"I assume you'll want to see your mother first?"

I nod, and we head to the hospital. It's a bit of a culture shock, being back in Portland. The city is too loud, too bright, too *different*. I'm wearing my old clothes, and Fen's trench coat, and I have my cell phone. I changed once we got to the mansion. So did Fen, who still looks wild and untamed. I feel more like myself than I've felt in the last few weeks, but less at home. It makes no sense to me.

I text Es on the way to the hospital.

Hey girl. I have a layover here for a few hours. Am checking on my mom and hoped we could meet for coffee?

Her reply is nearly instant.

Omgomgomgomg I've missed the hell out of you! Where are they keeping you locked up? No phone? No internet? No love?

Fen is reading over my shoulder and frowns. "You cannot tell her the truth."

I roll my eyes at him. "No kidding."

Not locked up. Just super busy. We are doing international meetings, lots of no-internet zones, but mostly just buried in books and research. Omg so much research. My head might explode from it all.

Not totally a lie, either. Reading by candlelight until all hours of the night isn't great for the head.

Can't wait to see you. Come by Roxy after seeing mom. I'll take a break. Everyone else would love to see you 2.

I smile.

Will do. Have someone for you to meet too. <3

I put my phone away as we park, knowing Es will be dying from suspense. I don't even bother checking the bajillion messages, texts and phone calls she and Pete have been leaving. My Facebook has blown up with too many tags and comments to check. Who knew I was so popular until I disappeared, literally, from the face of the earth.

My mom has been moved to a private room in the long term care wing, as promised by Asher, and I confirm with the nurse on duty that she is getting the best care available. When we enter her room, it is filled with fresh flowers and the curtains are open to let in some light. "I wonder who sent the flowers."

I check for a card, but there isn't one. Fen clears his throat, like he's guilty of something. "I asked Asher to have them sent regularly, so she'd have something fresh and pretty in her room."

I suck in a breath and try to keep the tears from welling in my eyes at his thoughtfulness. I surprise him with a hug, resting my head on his chest. His arms wrap around me somewhat reluctantly as I thank him.

His reply is gruff and self-conscious, and I pull away to see my mom.

She looks well enough, all things considered. Her color is good and all her machines seem to be clicking along as they are meant to. I take her hand, and she feels colder than I imagined. My fingers trace the outline of her demon mark that matches mine. "Hi, Mom. It's me, Ari. Are you doing okay?"

I know she won't respond, but I talk to her anyways, telling her things I'm not supposed to tell anyone, but she's unconscious and can't hear, and even if she could, she made a deal with a demon, so she obviously knows about this stuff. Fen doesn't stop me, so I just talk and talk until I can't think of anything else to say.

We've been there for hours when Fen checks his watch. "We should be going if you want to see your friends."

It's hard to say goodbye, knowing it will be another month before I can see her again. Knowing it will be seven months before she will be free of this curse. But I kiss her head and walk out with Fen by my side.

He takes my hand again. To comfort, of course, but I appreciate it nonetheless.

We take the limo to The Roxy, and though it's the busiest time of night, everyone on duty makes time to say hi. Es is most excited as she hangs up her black apron and shouts that she's leaving for a bit.

She keeps hugging me and grabbing my hands, while simultaneously trying to wipe tears away without messing up her makeup as we walk along the dark streets of Portland. "Girl, I have missed you. You can't even know how much."

I sniffle back my own tears and smile. "I've missed you too. Es, I'd like you to meet Fen. Fen this is Es, my best friend."

Es studies the man next to me, her eyebrow raised high. She holds out her hand for a kiss, and he obliges. She giggles and claps. "Oh Fen, it's such a *pleasure* to meet you. Tell me, do you work with Ari?"

"In a manner of speaking, yes."

"You know the guy who was here offering me the job?" I ask, speaking of Asher.

"How could I *ever* forget that tall drink of water?"

"He and Fen are brothers."

I swear Es is about to faint. "You know if I wasn't spoken for, I'd be asking if there are more where you boys came from."

I laugh. There are indeed five more, and I have to marry one.

"How are you, Es? What's been going on?" I don't have a lot of time left, so I have to cram as much BFF bonding in as I can.

"We miss you," she says. "A lot. But things are going well. Living at your place has been an absolute godsend. Thank you for that."

I smile, glad it's helping her.

Then she stops walking and clasps my hands. "And the best news of all...I have enough for my surgery. It's scheduled for next month. I'm hoping you can come back for it."

I hug her and squeal. "That's amazing news. I'm so happy for you." Then I frown and pull away. "Es, I don't know if I can be there. I'll try though, I swear."

Es glances to Fen then back to me. "You know, I keep up the smiles and banter because I love you. But I'm not a fool, Ari. I know when I'm being lied to. What's really going on?"

I suck in a breath and kick myself for being such a fool. Of course I couldn't pull this off without Es knowing something was up. Fen glares at me as if I need further warning not to spill the secret beans. "I'm okay, Es, I swear. It's...complicated, but what I'm doing is helping my mom."

I'm wearing a coat that covers my wrists, but as Es holds my hands her fingers slide over my raised mark. She pulls my sleeve up and stares. "What is this? This is like your mom's!"

I yank my hand back and cover the mark with Fen's coat. "It's nothing. Nothing you should worry about."

Es steps back, her expression one of betrayal and hurt. She walks over to Fen and points at his chest. "Is this your doing? Are you hurting her?"

"Es, he's not hurting me, he's helping me," I say, trying to push between the two of them. I give Fen a warning glare and he nods, seeming to understand my best friend is off limits.

Es looks to me again. "You've changed," she says. "It's like you're a stranger." She turns away, toward a bar with a glowing red open sign. She puts her hand on the door. "I'm going to use the ladies' room to regain my composure. Excuse me."

I stand, stunned, as she enters the bar, leaving us alone on the sidewalk.

"If she figures out the truth, she will be in danger," Fen says.

I swipe at a tear. "No one is to know she suspects something, and I won't tell her a thing. She's to be left alone, Fen. She's the only other family I have besides my mother."

Fen nods. "I will not tell. But be careful with her, Ari."

"I will."

We wait a while longer, but something isn't right. She's taking too long. Fen follows me into the crowded bar, and I navigate to the back alley where the bathrooms are. The air smells of cigarettes and booze.

Three beefy men surround Es. Their words are slurred and their steps wobbly. The biggest pushes against her. "Hey tranny, let's see your pecker!"

"I don't think you have the right parts for this bathroom, sheman," another says.

"Back off," I shout at them.

They don't see Fen yet. He's hidden by the shadows. So they laugh.

Big mistake.

Fen steps out of the darkness. They step back.

"What's going on here?" Fen growls.

The biggest, who seams to be the leader, smirks. "Can't you see for yourself? This freak's trying to get into the girl's room. Probably to molest and rape someone."

Fen steps forward. "What I see is a lady trying to use the bathroom. And pathetic excuses for men trying to stop her." He looks at Es. "Go ahead and use the bathroom. I'll have a chat with our new friends here."

Es looks at me, and I nod and join her in the bathroom.

There are thuds outside. Screams and yells. I don't know what Fen does to those guys, but they are gone when we come back out. Es walks over to Fen, and I hold my breath waiting.

She holds out her hand. "Thank you."

They shake. "You're welcome. You deserve to be treated like the lady you are."

I think Es is going to cry. I know I am.

Is it any wonder I'm falling for this man?

We walk Es back to The Roxy, and as we are about to leave she pulls me into a hug. "I won't say a word to anyone. Not even Pete. I don't know what's going on, but that man is in love with you, so I know he'll keep you safe."

I choke back a sob. "I love you, Es. I'm sorry."

She wipes a tear from my eye. "Love you too, girl. Be safe."

When we return to the limo, I feel more homesick than ever. But the home I'm missing is Stonehill, not Portland.

12

OUTLANDS

"Daison, I'd like you to meet Princess Arianna,
guest of Prince Fenris. Princess, this is my speaks-
before-thinking apprentice, Daison."
—Kayla Windhelm

It takes another three days before my sword is finally done. It seems surreal that I helped make the beauty I hold in my hands. Kayla grins like a fool. "You did an amazing job, Ari."

I look up at her and smile. "I really think this was more you than me. But thank you."

I worked the pendant stone Es gave me into the hilt, and Kayla helped me etch elaborate designs into the steel, so it wouldn't just be a stab and swipe kind of blade, but a real work of art.

I slide it into its custom black scabbard and practice drawing the sword. It hangs from one side of my hip, with the dagger Daison made on the other.

The boy stands in the shadows, beaming. He's become more comfortable with me recently, and we've fallen into a camaraderie that I enjoy. "You're a natural at blacksmithing," he says.

I'm about to argue, but Kayla cuts me off. "He's right. You have a gift for this. I hope you keep practicing when you leave."

I don't like thinking about leaving Stonehill, but my month will be up soon. I'm supposed to go to Dean next. Kayla knows how I feel about that, and she squeezes my hand. "This too shall pass," she says. "And then you can choose from your heart."

"You know I can't." My breath hitches. "You know he doesn't want this."

"My brother has a lot of secrets that keep him trapped in his own darkness. You might be the one who can help him into the light. Don't give up on him just yet."

I nod and push away unhappy thoughts as I swing my sword, practicing the moves Fen has drilled into me over weeks of training. I have muscles where none existed before, at least none you could see. I even have abs. I'm quite impressed with myself, to be honest.

"What's its name?" Daison asks.

"What?"

"Your sword. Every proper sword needs a name. What will you call yours?"

I raise the blade, admiring the swirls and eagles etched into the steel. "Spero. It means hope."

"Fitting," says Kayla.

Daison shrugs. "I would have gone with Dragonslayer or Heartbreaker personally."

I sheathe Spero and sigh. "Do you mind if I beg off today?"

Kayla laughs. "Let me guess, you want to show your sword off to Fen?"

I blush. I'm too easy to read. "Yeah. Basically."

She shoves me out of the smithy. "Go. Show off. You deserve it. But I'll expect you back here tomorrow ready to work."

I salute her in mock seriousness. "Yes, ma'am."

She rolls her eyes at me. "Cheeky girl. Get gone."

I walk quickly back to the castle, enjoying the weight of steel at my hip. I feel like a kid at Christmas and can't wait to share my excitement with Fen.

He's in the training arena talking to his soldiers when I approach.

His eyes fall to my hip, and he raises that one sexy eyebrow with the scar. The soldiers leave us, and he walks to me. "It is finished?"

"Yes!" I draw Spero and hand it to him to examine.

He studies the design, then raises the blade and considers its weight and balance before handing it back to me. "You did well. It's a perfect fit for you. Are you ready to begin training with real steel now?"

I nod.

He grins. "Very well. Prepare yourself." He pulls out his sword, and our blades clash together as he takes me through one of our sparring forms.

I can feel the difference in using a real sword versus wood, and I know I'm going to need to get even stronger to be a decent fighter. Working in the forge has helped build muscle, but I need more stamina than I have. I know I have untapped potential in me. I just need to push harder.

I'm sweating hard when a messenger runs at us, as if being chased by lions. "Prince Fenris! You must help! The Fae. They're at the walls."

My heart drops into my gut. I freeze, but not Fen. He's already shouting commands, rallying troops.

He turns to me and grips my arms so hard they will bruise. "Get into the castle and barricade yourself until I come back. I'm sending Roco and Marco with you for protection."

"No, Fen. I'm not going to hide when people in Stonehill need help. I'll find Kayla. We can evacuate the city while you and your soldiers fight off the attack."

He frowns. "You are too important to risk."

"I'm not a piece of property, and I'm not a political prop to use when it suits you," I argue. "I make my own choices."

"I could have you locked in your room until I return." He looks serious, and I can tell he's worried.

"Fen, listen to me carefully. If you lock me away, the consequences will not easily be undone."

He places a hand on my shoulder. "And if you die or get hurt, *those* consequences will undo me. Do not die, Princess."

"I won't."

He finally nods. "Fine, but stay within the city walls. There's a secret way out through the mountains. Kayla will know where it is. Get them out and get to safety. I'll find you."

I consider whether I should use my horse or just run, and I decide on running. Kayla's forge isn't that far away, and I won't have time to deal with my horse.

Heavy snow falls from the sky. It crunches under my feet as I retrace the steps I took just a few hours ago.

My mind is focused as I approach the center of the city. Fen's soldiers take formation at the gates and archers line the walls. I run to Kayla's forge and fill her in on what's happening. She looks at Daison, who has dropped his tongs. "Ring the bell and alert the people," Kayla says. "We need to get everyone out."

When he's gone, she pulls a leather bag from her counter and begins filling it with bandages, vials and jars she keeps on a shelf in case of injury. "Hand me that one over there," she says, pointing to a jar filled with brown sludge on the shelf behind me. I hand it to her.

"We must hurry," she says. "Go help Daison round up the people. We must lead them through the mountain pass quickly. There is a storm brewing tonight. If we aren't fast enough, we will be snowed in." She shoves the bag at me as she fills another one. "Keep this with you, just in case."

I take it from her. "I'm on it!" I run out and find Daison.

He rings the city bell and yells for people to hurry. "We haven't much time. Raiders are coming!"

That gets them moving faster, and buzz begins to spread. The Fae from the Outlands are here. They are here to kill and steal and rape.

To hurry things along, I go door to door, sharing the news as quickly as possible, helping pack when needed, carrying babies and guiding young children while their parents pack. As I do, I get small glimpses into these cloistered lives. I see the things they value most and the things they are willing to leave behind to burn, if it comes to that. They are a practical people, for the most part, choosing food, clothing, bedding, but almost everyone also has a sentimental item or two they can't leave behind. A special book, a cherished piece of jewelry. One woman brought her husband's old shaving kit, though he's been dead for many years now. "I can't leave it behind," she told me. "It still smells of him."

I can't bear to think this magical crystal city might be gone by nightfall, if Fen and his soldiers can't keep the raiders out. And I realize I don't understand war at all. I don't understand fighting and bloodshed and the need to kill others who are different from you. I know the Fae see themselves as the heroes of their own stories. We all do, don't we? But how can they justify what they are about to do? This village isn't full of soldiers. It's full of normal everyday people. Families just trying to get through their lives.

Kayla leads a long line of people towards the side of the castle. There, behind a waterfall, lies the mountain passage. I run up to the blacksmith, out of breath. In the distance, the sounds of battle thunder. The clash of steel. The last screams of dying men.

"Where's Daison?" Kayla asks.

"I thought he was with you? I was helping others prepare to evacuate."

She pauses, as people pass by her into the side of the mountain. It's snowing again, and the wind is blowing more forcefully than before. The cold chills me through my cloak and clothing, and I shiver, startled at how fast the storm is growing.

"We have to get out of here," she says. "I'm going to find Daison. You lead everyone."

She turns to leave, but I grab her hand. "Kayla, I don't know the way. Only you do. I'll find Daison, and we'll catch up to you. He's probably just helping someone pack."

I see the indecision in her eyes, but she relents, knowing I'm right. "Ari, please find him."

"I will. See you soon."

I run back towards the city just as burning arrows fly over the wall and land in bushes and barns and houses. Fires begin to rage out of control.

I run faster, calling for Daison, worry gnawing at me the longer it takes to find him.

Flames rise up around me. Smoke chokes me. I pull my shirt over my mouth and keep looking for the boy.

"Daison! Where are you?"

I hear a moan from behind and turn around. A pile of burning wood. A foot sticking out. "Daison!"

I look around for something I can use to move the rubble without burning myself, and settle on a wooden plank near a half finished house. I grab the board, a rusty nail digging into my skin. I ignore the pain, and rush back to Daison. All around me is chaos. Fire. Smoke. The smell of burning flesh.

I ram the plank under the burning logs and push down. The wood tumbles toward me, spraying me with embers, singeing my hands. I bite down in pain, and realize I bit my tongue. Warm blood fills my mouth.

I block out the burn between my jaws, the fire on my hands. I jam the plank forward, moving away more wood. Sparks hit me. This time, I don't flinch. I shove the board forward again. The last of the wood rolls away.

I drop the burning plank and grab Daison by the feet. His body is blackened by fire. Part of his face has melted away. He smells of cooked meat. "Oh Daison."

I don't know what else to do. I pull off my cloak and use it to pack snow around his body to cool the burns and numb him.

His eyes flicker open. "Ari..." His voice is a cracked whisper. I lean down closer to hear him. "Ari, a little girl is trapped. Help. Her."

He coughs and his body spasms. For a moment, I am frozen, my hands numb. Then I run to the burning house and yell for anyone who might be inside. I hear a girl scream, and I rush in, covering my body with my arms. The girl sits in the stone fireplace, one of the only places not on fire. I reach for her. "Come to me. I'm here to help."

She shakes her head, her pink curls bobbing around her pointed ears.

"Sweetie, I can't reach you in there. Come on out and let's find your parents."

Slowly, she crawls out. I grab her hand and pull her into my arms. I rush outside, flaming wood falling behind me. We get back to Daison. His body still shakes and spasms.

"I've got her, Daison. Now we need to get you both to Kayla and out of the city."

"I can't, Ari. Save the girl."

I hold his hand, the one not burned, my throat constricting. "No, this isn't over. You'll make it!"

"Tell Kayla..." He chokes and blood stains his lips. "Tell her it's not her fault. She's family. Always."

His eyes close and his chest stills and my heart breaks, all in the same moment.

I don't know what to do. I can't leave him here, but I have to get the girl to safety. The city is burning.

I check Daison's pulse three times. Then I cover his face with my cloak and look at the girl. He died trying to save her. And I will die too, if I must.

I stand, tears staining my face, and grab the girl into my arms. I carry her past the smoke and rubble. I carry her to the waterfall by the castle. I do not know how long it takes. I only know that I must succeed. When I reach the stone steps, I glance down and see Daison in my arms. But it is just a vision. A trick cast by madness and sorrow.

This world cares nothing for me.

It cared nothing for Daison.

I am half conscious. Half mad.

And then I hear it.

Water. Splashing.

I fall to my knees behind the waterfall, and the girl drops to the ground. Someone takes her hand and pulls her toward the tunnel. They try to lift me up. They cannot. They yell. They take the girl and disappear. I sit there for minutes, hours, eternity.

Something licks my hand. Nudges my head.

"Baron?"

He growls.

Slowly, my head grows clearer. "What's going on, boy?"

Baron whines in a way I've never heard before. He scratches his paws on the ground. "I don't understand what you want me to do, buddy. Is it Fen? Is he okay?"

War cries bleed through the wails of wind and snow. A bluster of snow swirls around me and Baron. I shiver and try to pull my cloak tighter. It's no longer there. It's still wrapped around Daison.

Baron takes a few steps towards the gate.

I hesitate.

He looks over his shoulders, checking to see if I'm coming, then walks again. I have no idea where he wishes to go, but I know in my gut I must follow.

13

STORM OF BLOOD

"I would have gone with Dragonslayer or Heartbreaker personally."

—Daison

Baron leads me higher up the mountain, to a small tunnel in the stone. "I really hope you know what you're doing, Baron."

I have to hold onto him and let him guide me in the darkness. My mind flashes with images of Daison, where I left him by the waterfall.

I push away the memory and focus on my steps, on the sound of dripping water. We step out of the tunnel and into a graveyard. The dead litter the ground: the soldiers of Stonehill clad in white and red armor, the raiders covered in brown and grey furs. In the distance, past a fog of white snow, Fen's soldiers chase the Fae through the forest. We won, and yet the city is destroyed.

Baron guides me through the red snow, away from the city. We enter a forest, where the branches are thick and the sky is dark though there are no more leaves. I have never been here before.

The sun is setting now. Twilight is descending upon us, bringing with it more snow and sub-zero temperatures. Baron seems fine with the cold. I'm freezing, but I keep moving. Something is wrong. I can feel it like a shackle around my gut.

Twenty minutes into our hike, Baron's ears twitch and he stops, a low growl in his throat. A moment later, I hear what the wolf heard first.

Men. Talking. I crouch next to Baron and listen.

"He'll tell us soon enough. Lester, here, can get anyone talking. Even a prince." My stomach drops.

And then I smell flesh burning, and I turn and release whatever was in my stomach as silently as I can.

"Why don't he yell? Anyone else would be screaming!" A different voice.

"Would you both shut the hell up?" A third voice says. "I'm trying to work. He'll scream eventually. They always do."

A picture forms in my mind. I want to reject the images. It can't be true. I creep closer, fear knotting my gut. Three men bundled in furs sit by a fire. In front of them stands a large rock. A man is chained to the stone, his mouth gagged with a rag.

The man is Fen.

I can't breathe. Can't see straight. I want to charge forward and save him, but I have to be smart. Even Baron knew he couldn't take on all three armed men at once and live.

So I take a deep breath and observe as many details as possible.

The three are armed. One of them, Lester, I presume, has a sharp prong that he sticks in the fire and brings to Fen's bare chest. He yanks the cloth from Fen's mouth. "Do you want to tell me now? If not we can keep going. I'm enjoying this a lot more than you are, right about now."

Fen spits on his face, and the man scowls and lays iron on skin, leaving a burning red mark. Fen's face twitches, but he doesn't make a sound.

"It's like he's made of marble. What the hell?" That's the second man I heard speaking. He's lanky with red hair and a red beard.

"Settle yourself, Cliff. Have some patience." The man speaking is big and tall, a brutish man with thick orange hair.

Lester is the most refined of the bunch. Slender with cropped white hair and a handsome face. They are all Fae.

I know you can't judge an entire people by a few—the girls who work for me are Fae and lovely—but these men...I want to skewer them all for what they are doing to Fen.

Why doesn't he fight back? Tear them apart? How did they capture him to begin with?

"At least the raiders did their part," says Cliff. "Brought him to us like a present."

So the whole thing was just a trap to capture Fen. But why? Why not just come after me directly if that's what they were going for?

Doesn't matter. We have to save him. I've got a sword and a very angry wolf. That will have to be enough. Now I just need a plan.

I'm still trying to think of something when Lester summons Cliff, who groans but comes to stand beside him, holding out his wrist. Lester slashes Cliff's skin with a knife and sticks the bloody arm over Fen's mouth. Why are they feeding him blood? Wouldn't that make him stronger? I feel like I'm in one of those nightmares where you have no idea what's going on, but everyone expects you to know what to do.

Fen tries to pull away from the blood, to refuse it, but Lester holds his head and shoves the blood into his mouth, forcing it on him. When Cliff pulls away, Fen's eyes are heavy, and his head lulls to the side, his body slumped in his chains.

"The ultimate irony, isn't it?" Lester taunts with a cruel smile. "Your kind coming to our world, only to find we are poison to you. But it's a sweet poison, isn't it? One you want more of."

Cliff holds his arm up, and Fen looks up, his nostrils sniffing at the blood, his eyes crazed with desire. This time when Cliff offers Fen his wrist, Fen doesn't resist. Not at first, but then a spark returns to his eyes, and he jerks his head away, spitting the blood out.

Lester paces in front of him. "You are stronger than most of your kind. Even of the first, you are something special, aren't you? But I'll find a way to break you. In fact, I think I've already found it."

The other man. The big one with orange hair is gone.

I was too focused on Fen, on figuring out a way to stop his torture to notice.

I spin around. The big man is there, a few feet away, sword in hand. Baron jumps forward. The man kicks him away.

I clutch the hilt of my sword, but before I can draw Spero, the man grabs my arm. With his other hand he grabs my hair and yanks me toward his group.

A gust of wind rips through the sky. The snow is thick. It's hard to see in front me.

Cliff tucks his hands into his coat, his wrist now bandaged. "We need to wrap this up, or we'll die out here."

"Be silent, Cliff. We have the bitch we came for, but I need one more thing from our prince before we kill him." Lester motions me closer. I fight, but the giant man twists my hands behind my back and pushed me forward. Lester holds a knife to my throat.

Fen struggles against his chains, his rage feral. "Let her go, or you will know pain you cannot imagine."

"Tell me what I need to know and I will not hurt her. Fail to tell me, and she dies." Lester pushes the knife against my throat hard enough to break skin. I feel the blood drip onto my collarbone. He turns back to the prince.

"I'm sorry, Fen," I say. "I should have acted sooner."

His eyes are frantic. His body rages against the restraints. But he cannot break free. He cannot save me.

This time, I must save us both.

I twist, pulling the giant man off balance. He crashes to the ground. I draw Spero and plunge the blade into his back. It goes in smoothly. Quietly.

A part of me knows I have taken a life. It whispers to me of guilt and shame. But right now, I cannot listen. My mind thunders with rage. And there are more lives to take.

I charge at Cliff. Blade forward. His sword is up in defense. I feign a strike from above, but attack from below, slicing his knees. He falls, screaming and staining the snow red.

Baron jumps forward from behind me, landing on Cliff's chest, slashing at the man's throat until he screams no more.

Fen roars, fighting against his restraints, but he isn't strong enough to break free. Lester's eyes widen, glancing between his fallen comrades and me. He holds a knife in one hand, a hot poker in the other.

I strike at his feet.

He blocks low, crouching. And that is when I have him. There is more to a sword than just the blade. That I learned from Kayla.

I rush my hand up.

And slam my pommel into Lester's face.

He falls backwards, his nose broken and red.

Baron stalks forward.

The man pleads for his life. He looks to me. "Stop him. Stop him, please."

My mind is cold. My heart quiet. "You harmed Fenris Vane, Prince of War. Perhaps I would spare you, but he will not."

Baron leaps forward.

And the man pleads no more.

I run over to his body and grab a key from his belt. I find a lock on the chains and open it. The metal falls.

I rush to Fen and drop to my knees before him, tears streaming down my face. "Are you okay?" I ask.

He shakes his head. "I've been poisoned. It's working its way through my body right now. It will take too long to leave my system. We need to find shelter before this storm buries us. I'd survive, but you..." He takes my hand and pulls me closer to him. "You wouldn't make it out here."

Baron walks over to us, then howls long and loud into the night.

I help Fen stand, but he has to lean heavily on me to walk. "Where do we go?" I ask.

Fen looks at Baron. "Find us a cave, boy. Someplace out of the storm."

Baron howls again, not as long this time, and begins sniffing around. He takes off, slowing when he realizes we aren't following as quickly as we should be.

It's slow going, and I'm so very cold. Fen is getting worse, his body heavier with each step. I'm worried I won't be able to keep going, that I'll get too cold and my body will collapse under the weight of us both, but just as I'm about to lose hope, Baron howls again and disappears into darkness. I follow him, hoping it's some kind of shelter, and find a cave carved into the side of a mountain. I assume Baron already checked for unfriendly critters, so I duck and put a hand over Fen's head to protect him from knocking himself silly as we scoot into the cave.

I can barely see inside. We'll need a fire for light and to survive the cold. Or at least I'll need a fire. My vampire might be fine, but he doesn't look fine, and I'm not okay with him suffering.

I lower him carefully to the floor. The cave is bigger inside than the opening makes it seem.

Fen groans and tries to stand, but I push against his chest and he stays. "No moving. You need to rest. I'm going to find some wood and build a fire. Just...sit."

"Don't go out," he says. "The storm is coming."

"I'll take Baron and stay close to the cave, but I need heat even if you don't."

He tries to stand again. "I'll get it."

I push him back like he's a child. "Shut up. You aren't going anywhere, and I'm not helpless. Just don't make more work for me by trying to be a tough guy and hurting yourself more."

I leave before he can argue more. Baron stays at my heels, and I scavenge through snow that freezes my hands, trying to find dry enough wood to burn. When I have an armful, I return to the cave and set up the fire pit the way Fen taught me during one of our training sessions. He felt it was important I learn more than just fighting, that I learn some survival skills as well, given how unfamiliar this world is to me. I grumbled at the lessons then, but silently bless him for them now.

It takes me longer than I'd like, and I let fly a few choice curse words when I come close to getting the fire going only to repeatedly fail, but finally a tiny ember sparks. I stack more tinder on the flame, then fan it with my hand so it ignites. The blaze grows until it's a proper campfire, and I sit back and grin, proud of myself.

The cave lights up with the glow of flames, and I scoot closer to Fen to examine his wounds. He's still without a shirt, and his skin is on fire, not cold as I expected. "What did he do to you?" I ask.

Fen places his hand on my face, his blue eyes locked on mine. "Nothing that some rest won't fix. I'll be okay. You shouldn't have come. How did you even find me? Why didn't you escape with the city like I told you?"

"Baron came for me, and I knew something was wrong. I knew you were in trouble."

"You stubborn, stubborn woman. You could have gotten yourself killed."

I touch the stubble on his cheek, my eyes filling with tears. "But I didn't. You were the one who came too close to dying tonight."

He laughs, then coughs for his effort, covering his mouth as he does. When he pulls away, his palm is covered in blood. I grab it and stare, horrified. "Coughing up blood is really bad, Fen. What did they do to you?"

He wipes his hand on the ground and straightens himself. "Fae blood is poison to vampires. It won't kill us. Very few things will actually kill us. But it weakens us and makes us very sick, often for a long time."

"How do you treat it?"

He looks away. "We have to feed on a human to cleanse our blood from the Fae."

I don't even hesitate. I offer my wrist to him. "Then do it. Drink my blood and heal."

He shakes his head. "Even if I was willing to feed from you, which I'm not, it's been forbidden. None of us can feed from you until you've taken the Blood Oath."

"Then I'll find a vampire you can feed on."

"You would freeze to death in this storm, firstly. And second, while vampires can feed on each other, it doesn't give us the nourishment that human blood gives us. It can help us heal from certain wounds though, which is useful, but not something like this."

"Then you need to feed on me. Who forbade it? It's my blood and my right to give it to whom I choose."

"Let's talk about this in the morning," he says, his body too limp under my hands. "You need to rest."

"Now who's being the stubborn one, huh?"

"I'm not being stubborn, there are just things at play here you don't understand." He flinches as he adjusts himself against the stone, and I grab the bag Kayla prepared. "Your wounds need tending. Stay still."

He grabs my hand. "They will heal in time."

"But they aren't healing now," I say. "So I need to clean and bandage them so they don't get infected, or whatever happens to vampires when they are injured."

I pull out bandages and a cream meant for cuts, scrapes and burns. We get a lot of those at the forge. Fen doesn't show any expression as I inspect the wounds on his chest, my fingers prying gently to make sure he's not getting an infection. I use some snow and a cloth to wipe away any extra debris from the forest and then apply a thick layer of cream over each wound before securing it with a bandage. "So what things are at play that I don't understand?" I ask as I work.

"You ask a lot of questions," he says.

I roll my eyes at him. "Yeah, I'm irritating that way, always wanting to know things that have a direct impact on my life and well-being. Must be a silly human thing."

"You're right," he says. "It does affect you. And you'll need to be careful. My brothers and I have been around a very long time. You couldn't even fathom how long if you tried. We have seen the rise and fall of many empires and kingdoms and we have fought many wars. We have killed more than you can imagine. We have done horrible things, deserving of our demon curse. These are the men you will be spending time with in the coming months. These are your choices for the next king. We are dangerous, Ari. More than you know. And there are some who would stop at nothing to become the next king. When you are dealing with an immortal species, you don't often see change in leadership except by violence, and even then, we are hard to kill, as I've said. What is happening now is unprecedented. And you are at the center of it all. The High Council decided on rules to keep you safe."

"Like no feeding from me."

He nods. "Yes. However, other things were left open. And that's where you have to be careful."

"Other things like what?" I ask, securing the last bandage.

"There are no limits on physical intimacy," he says, glancing away.

My hand freezes on his chest. Our faces are just a few inches apart. Outside, the snow falls so fast and hard it turns the world into a cacophony of shrills and howls, dimmed only slightly by the crackling fire in our small cave. Baron sleeps next to us, his body close to the flame for warmth, but his head facing the cave's entrance, presumably to keep guard. All of this registers in an instant, but none of it matters, because all I can feel is the pressure of this man's hand on my hip, his fingers gripping me harder than necessary. "So anything goes then?"

"Essentially, yes."

"With my consent, of course."

"With me that would always be true, but that's not the case with others."

"So they would force me?" My voice quivers at the thought of the violation. "How do they think that will convince me to choose them in the end?"

"If they can impregnate you first, then they will have to be the one you choose. The heir must come first."

"So if I get pregnant, I have no choices left?"

His hand squeezes my hip. "Correct. That's why Levi isn't worried about his earlier display. He doesn't need you to like him. He just needs you to carry his child. Also, there are other ways to manipulate you into sex that aren't so…clearly forced, but which you would still consider a violation of the consent that is so important to you."

I frown. "Ways like what? Drugs?"

"In a manner of speaking. You've experienced the effect Dean had on you. He is the demon of lust and he can make you want things…feel things…that would be hard not to act on." Fen turns his head away from me, his jaw clenched.

I put a hand on his cheek, feeling the stubble of hair on my skin as I pull his face up to look at me. "Dean can use all his tricks on me, but I am not ruled by desire or lust. I'm smarter than that. And I gotta say, his recent alignment with Levi left him low on my list. I felt nothing when near him that night."

"They are strong, Ari. Powerful. We are the Fallen. The first of our kind to come to this world. The original cursed. You wouldn't stand a chance against them. Against any of us."

A buzz grows between us. This electric charge I can't pull away from. "Then you'll have to stick around and protect me. That's your job, isn't it?"

"Yes." His voice is deeper than normal. More gravelly.

"Then don't leave me," I whisper. "I know it's only been a few weeks, but I can't imagine being in this world without you. You have become my rock."

"Oh, Arianna. You don't know what you're asking of me."

"Then tell me. Help me understand. Am I wrong in thinking what I'm feeling between us is mutual?"

He pulls me closer to him, our bodies now pressed together. I can feel the heat of his skin through my clothes. He's so feverish. So sick. I shouldn't be pushing him like this, but I can't let him slip away from me, and that's what I fear will happen if I don't break through this wall he's put up between us.

"You are not wrong." He uses one hand to cup my cheek. His gaze is penetrative, and I stay still, my breath threading through me in the smallest of movements, my body on fire, every nerve hyper-alert.

I see so much in his blue eyes. So many years of living. So much pain. So much sadness. But also so much strength. So much kindness. So much untapped tenderness. I want more than anything to reach into his soul and pull it out of the self-imposed darkness and into the light.

He leans in and presses his lips to mine. I shiver as our mouths connect. His hand moves from my face to the back of my head as he buries his fingers in my hair and pulls me closer. His other hand wraps around my waist and splays against my back. I let myself relax into his body, as I straddle his lap, my chest pressed against his, my arms wrapping around his neck.

The kiss deepens, taking on a life of its own as our bodies come to life with each other. Our breath merges, and the urgency of our need dances through our skin, infecting us with wild abandon.

I grip his neck harder, my fingers tugging on his hair, my desire clawing through me like a starving creature in need of air, life.... him.

He tastes of mint leaves, and his scent is wild, earthy. I can't get enough of him, of this, of everything I feel when I'm with him.

His hands explore my body, and I push myself closer to him, adjusting myself on top of him. I know he wants me as much as I want him.

Now. Here. In the middle of a storm. In a cave by a fire.

He moves from my mouth to my neck and ear, kissing, nibbling, sucking. I groan against him, my face buried in his neck. He lifts me effortlessly and repositions us so that I'm on my back. He leans over me, his body pressed between my legs. His hair falls around his face as he looks at me in the firelight. "We do not have to do this."

I reach up to grip his neck and pull his face to mine. "I want you, Fenris Vane. Now."

A growl rumbles deep in his throat, and he kisses me again. His body is hot. Too hot.

Something is wrong.

He pulls away and rolls onto his back. He starts to shake. His throat is tight. He's choking!

I sit up and lean over him. "Fen! What's wrong?"

His body convulses, and he coughs up foam and blood. His eyes lose focus, and he grows paler.

"Fen! What do I do? What's happening?"

"The poison," he says through crimson lips. "Something in the blood."

Oh god. He looks about to pass out, or worse. Baron comes over to us, whining and growling. He lies next to his master and places his large paws on Fen's chest, then looks up at me with such a human expression of sadness, fear and pleading my heart nearly breaks.

I look around for something sharp and find a small knife in my pack. I hold my wrist over Fen's mouth, take a deep breath, and slice my skin open with the blade.

The cut is deep. I clench my jaw to not cry out in pain. But the blood is flowing. I push it closer to his mouth.

He has lost all reason. His eyes are closed. He no longer moves.

"Drink my blood," I tell him, tears pooling in my eyes. There are ways to kill immortals, Fen told me. Did the raiders find one?

My blood dribbles out of his mouth. He's not taking it. "Drink!" I scream at him, pushing my wrist into his mouth and holding his head up with my other hand so the blood goes down his throat.

I don't know how long the bleeding will continue. I'm ready to cut my wrist again if he doesn't wake up.

I'm close to it, raising my dagger, when he moves, his mouth gripping on, sucking the blood out of me. It's working. He's waking up. He's drinking.

Now all I can do is pray this heals him before it kills me.

14

PRINCESS ARIANNA

"You are the chosen one, there is a prophecy, and
danger, and, of course, my sexy charms."

—Asher

I am cold. So cold. I can't stop shivering. I've wrapped my wrist, but the bandages keep bleeding through.

Our fire is dying, and we are nearly out of wood.

Fen's fever seems to have abated. His color is returning, and he's breathing well, but he hasn't woken. His wounds are healing though. Now I just have to find a way to not die of hypothermia while we wait out this storm and his recovery.

Baron stays by Fen's side, keeping him warm and watching over him like a worried mother.

I cross my arms over my chest in a vain attempt to warm myself by the meager fire. It won't take long to burn out and the storm still rages outside. Surely someone would have sent scouts out to look for us? But could they even travel in this weather?

I look down at the blood seeping through my bandages again and sigh. This wound won't heal quickly, but it might have saved Fen's life, so I have no regrets. This world, this kingdom, needs him.

I need him.

I also need more fire.

I stand and walk to the cave's opening. It looks miserable out there. A flurry of snow has piled at the exit to the point that we are almost trapped.

"Baron, I need your help to get out of here. We need more wood."

He comes over quickly, and I point to the snow blocking our escape.

He understands my intention and begins digging, making me a path. I follow him through to the other side. I have never felt so cold in my life as I crawl through a snow bank.

The world is completely covered in white. My only hope is to find a tree that has some lower branches I can break off to burn.

Baron moves to follow me, but I turn to him and shake my head, pointing back to the cave. "Guard Fen. Come find me if he gets worse."

Baron looks to me, then back at the cave, whining. I can see the uncertainty in his eyes. He wants to protect us both.

"It's okay, boy. I won't wander far. I'll be back in a minute. Just keep the entrance open for me."

Finally he turns to head back to the cave, and I wonder if I've made the right decision as my legs sink into thigh deep snow.

I feel like the answer is no. But Fen can't be left alone right now. And I remember a good tree not too far from here that should have some branches I can use.

Walking is laborious. I'm weak from blood loss, lack of food and cold. My limbs are frozen. But still I take one step in front of the other. The tree shouldn't be much further. It will have what I need, and I will go back to the cave, and it will feel positively toasty compared to this winter hell.

I might lose a few toes or fingers, but I'll live. That's the important thing. I wonder if my digits would grow back once I am turned into a vampire. That would be nice.

My mother's words run through my mind as I walk. *Dum spiro spero*. While I breathe, I hope. I am still breathing. I will not give up hope.

My mind wanders to my night with Fen before he passed out. Before I fed him my blood.

The way his mouth felt against mine. The way it felt to hold him and be held by him. Just the thought of it seems to warm me.

I see the tree just ahead and nearly cheer out loud with relief, but it feels too hard to open my mouth.

It takes a long time to reach the trunk, as slow as I'm walking, but when I do I'm happy to find that there are some branches that will work if I can break them off.

I focus on the smaller ones. I don't have the strength left to break thicker branches. Once I have as many as I can carry, I turn around and begin my slow plod back to the cave.

I try to imagine the heat of the fire, the comfort of being close to Fen as he sleeps and heals, the safety of having Baron there, anything to keep me from thinking about the cold seeping into my bones. Even my soul is freezing at this point.

The snowing stops, giving me a respite from the cold coming down upon me, and allows me to follow my trail back to the cave without getting lost. I just pretend that was my plan all along, that I wasn't worried about the snow filling in my tracks, me lost in the middle of a forest in the middle of a storm and dying as an icicle.

Without the sound of the storm whipping through the trees, it's a peaceful walk back. My arms burn from the weight of the wood. My wrist stings as the branches rub against my cut. But it's so breathtakingly beautiful and calm that I can almost forget about the pain.

It is because of this absolute stillness and silence that I hear them before they attack.

I drop my hard-earned wood into the snow and grip my sword's hilt, slowing my breathing so I can hear better.

They approach from my right. There's more than one person, but it doesn't sound like a big group.

I pull Spero out slowly, quietly, and make my way to a large tree to hide behind. It could be a search party looking for us. Someone from the castle here to help. I want to believe that's the case, that we will be rescued and taken back to warm Stonehill and all will be well.

But my gut says otherwise.

This isn't a rescue party.

It's the Fae coming for me.

They led us into this trap, bringing Fen out here. They are the only ones who know where he is.

I crouch behind a tree, sword ready.

I was smart enough to at least cut my left hand, so my sword arm still functions as well as it can in this weather.

But I am weak and tired and they are many. And I don't have Baron to help. My best chance is to hide. To not be found.

But what if they find Fen? What if they hurt him to find me? I won't let that happen. I'll surrender first.

I'm glad Baron is guarding him. If something happens to me, Fen will be safe. I can at least make sure of that.

Two men and a woman enter the clearing where I stood moments before. They are dressed in furs and leather and accompanied by a wolf. This one black and smaller than Baron. The wolf sniffs the ground, and then looks around.

"She's got to be somewhere close," the taller man says. He looks young, like all Fae, but his beard is long and grey. He carries a walking staff with a blue crystal molded into the top.

"It will be hard to get a scent in this snow," the woman says. She's nearly as tall as the man she speaks with. "We should have waited until after the storm cleared."

The shorter man looks into the sky and shakes his head. "This is our only chance. She is alone, unprotected by the demon she lives with. All the signs say we must act now."

They know so much. But how?

They circle the clearing, checking bushes and trees. It won't be long before they find my tracks, until they get to my tree. If I move or try to run, they will catch me. I'm paralyzed with fear.

The shorter man looks up suddenly, as if he heard something, but I haven't moved an inch. I'm barely breathing.

He smiles. "She's here. Somewhere close. She can hear us."

"Good," the woman says. "Then she will know we have only come to take her home. Princess Arianna, come out and show yourself. We are not the enemies you fear. We are your kin. Your true family." Her voice is full of authority, but I don't understand what she means.

"You do not belong with the demons who have tried to destroy our world," she says. "You are Fae. And you are the true ruler of this world."

Hands grab me from behind. "Found her!" It's the shorter man. He snuck up on me while the woman talked. This time, I am too weak to fight. He places a cloth over my face. "Sorry about this, Your Highness. But it's time to get you home."

...

When I awaken, I find myself slung over the shoulder of the tall man. I struggle free of his arms, and he drops me unceremoniously on the snow-packed ground of a wooded forest.

"Be gentle with her. She is not to be hurt," the woman says.

"She bit me," the tall man says, rubbing his arm where I did, indeed take a bite.

"Seems she learned more from the demons than we realized," the short man says with a chuckle.

The tall man glares at him, but I interrupt their bickering. "Who are you and where are you taking me?"

My hands and feet are tied together with rope, and I can't stand or do much but sit on the cold ground glaring at the three of them. My wrist is still bleeding, and with my hands behind my back, I rub my finger into the blood and draw on the earth. I know the symbol by heart, having traced it on Fen's wrist so many times.

If I can call to him through magic, maybe he can find me.

The woman approaches me before I can finish the symbol, and I shift my hands to cover it, so she doesn't see what I tried to do. I need them to lower their guard, so I can try again.

"I'm going to cut the ropes on your feet so you can walk," she says, "but if you fight me, you'll stay in the ropes, understand?"

I nod and watch as she pulls out a knife and frees my feet from the constraints.

She helps me stand, and I look around for a way to escape, but I have no idea where we are.

"You will freeze to death before ever finding help," the short man says.

I'm still wobbly from the drug they gave me, and my vision is blurry. The woman grips my arm and escorts me forward, to a cave carved into the side of a mountain. "To answer your question, we are taking you to your rightful kingdom."

"What are you talking about?"

The cave is large, much larger than the one Fen and I escaped into. Stalactites hang from the roof like menacing crystal weapons. They are beautiful in a cold, hard way.

"You will see soon enough," the woman says.

We walk deeper into the cave and reach a spacious cavern. Two towering blocks of stone stand as sentinels at the corners of a stone door. In the middle is an imprint in the shape of a hand with a small spike sticking out from the palm. The woman places her hand on it, impaling her skin. The handprint glows a bright white as she pulls away, and the intricate pattern inside runs with thin lines of her blood.

From within the structure something shifts and moves, metal mechanisms clicking into place, and then the door opens. The tall man nudges me into the stone box, and the others follow us in. The doors close, leaving us in utter darkness. The woman speaks a word I don't understand, and a ball of light forms just above us, glowing bright enough to illuminate the space.

Magic?

I don't have much time to consider, because the stone box we are in starts to move. I gasp and nearly fall, but the tall man catches my arm and holds onto me as we begin to sink into the ground.

"This is one of many secret passages that connect the two sides of our world, allowing us to travel between them with ease," the woman explains.

"Where is it taking us?" I ask, my voice falling flat in the confined space.

"You'll see," she says with a secret smile.

We begin to move faster and faster, and my stomach flips and topples until I feel like vomiting. I shuffle to one of the walls and lean against it, my shoulders aching from being pulled behind me.

"Did you kill the king?" I ask, thinking of Fen's investigation and the missing pieces he hasn't put together, like how the enemy gained access to High Castle. "Is this how you infiltrated the castle?"

"All your questions will be answered in time, but nothing is what you think. You have been deceived by the ultimate deceivers. The princes and their kind cannot be trusted."

The dungeon warden said something similar to me the day I arrived here, and while I certainly don't trust most of them, I think the Fae are wrong to judge them all. Still, the princes have my mother's soul, and I can't leave her at their mercy.

"I have to go back!" I say, my voice urgent. "My mother is their prisoner. If I don't fulfill my contract, her body on earth will die and her soul will be trapped in their dungeon forever." I can't sacrifice her like that. Fen would try to protect her, try to argue I was taken against my will, but demon contracts are not so easily violated.

"Your mother is not our concern," the tall man says.

The woman frowns at him. "What Gerard means to say is we will do everything we can to ensure the safety of your mother, but our first priority is getting you safely home."

Home. I know they don't mean earth. And they clearly don't mean the Kingdom of Inferna. So where is home? "You've got the wrong person. I'm just a normal girl trying to save my mom. I'm not your leader, or whoever you think I am."

They say nothing as our stone elevator moves faster.

I don't know how long the journey takes. My mind is still muddled with drugs. But at one point something changes, and I begin to float. We all do. My stomach turns, and I vomit. Bits of food glide in front of me.

I try to grab the wall but there's nothing to hold onto. The three Fae flip around so their feet point up.

"Do as we do," the woman says. "The gravity will shift in a moment and you will land on your head if you remain as you are."

I turn myself upside down just in time. When the gravity returns, we fall on what was once the ceiling. Now, we are moving up. Or down? Or...I don't know what just happened.

"Our kingdom is on the other side of this world," the woman says. "I would say bottom, if you imagine you've been living on the top. But really there is no bottom or top. It's all gravitationally irrelevant. We are now halfway home."

None of the maps I looked through indicated there was anything on the 'other side.' It looked like a floating island in the sky.

But if the woman is correct, and the princes don't know, they are in danger. They think the rebel Fae are isolated to the Outlands. They have no idea there's anyone living on the other side of the world.

I sit on the floor, my back against the stone, and try to process all my thoughts. My wrist is throbbing and my bandage is bleeding through, but I don't have any supplies on me, so I press my hand against the wound, hoping to stem the blood loss until we get where we are going.

The woman sees the bandage and frowns. "You were injured?"

I don't want to explain I was feeding a vampire, so I just nod. She sinks to her knees, cuts the ropes tying my hands together, and pulls my hand toward her, unwrapping the bandage as she does. "This is deep. We must heal it quickly. You've lost too much blood."

She pulls out a small knife and pricks her thumb, rubs a bit of blood on a green stone she takes from her pocket, then chants words in another language with her eyes closed until the stone begins to glow. With her eyes still closed, she presses the stone to my wound. It burns, and I bite my lip to keep from crying out. A deep ache spreads through my arm, and when I look down, the skin is knitting itself back together, healing the cut.

I feel lightheaded, and the woman looks paler than she had, but I'm no longer bleeding. There's not even a scar. "How did you do that?" Though I know the answer. I saw Kayla do nearly the same thing with Daison.

My heart drops at the thought of the sweet boy.

The woman smiles and slips the green stone back into a small leather pouch. "The magic is in our blood. In your blood. You will learn all of this and more."

While the idea of learning magic appeals to me, nothing they say can be trusted. I've seen how they attack the people I care for. How they burned an entire city, a city that included their own kind, just to lure me and Fen out. They are not my kin, and I will not be seduced by their empty promises.

The elevator finally stops, and the stone door opens, revealing a long tunnel lit with lanterns.

The glowing light above our heads disappears, and I follow the three of them through the tunnels.

The tall man has my sword strapped to his back, and I imagine taking it and fighting them all, but I'm still too weak. I have no idea where I am or how to get back to Fen. So I let them lead me until I can think of a better plan that might work. Maybe I can still draw the mark? I rub the ring Fen gave me as a talisman to give me luck and strength. I'm going to need both before this is over.

We walk through winding underground paths, then up stairs until we reach a giant cavern. Blue stalagmites hang from the ceiling, lighting the area. And before me stands a castle. More majestic than anything I've ever seen. It is made of crystal and marble with the most graceful and elegant design throughout. Tall spires rise high above, blending with the cavern's walls. The large gate is decorated with two white stags. It opens on its own.

I'm led inside, to a large hall with a wooden table in the center. It is covered with food and drink and at the head a man sits eating a piece of meat. He looks up and smiles when he sees me, then stands, arms out. "Princess Arianna, here at last. It is such a pleasure to finally meet you."

I know his face, but it's impossible. He can't be who I think he is.

"I know, it is quite a shock. I should be dead after all, but alas, as you can see, I'm very much alive."

"King Lucian? But, how?"

"I'm afraid that bit of trickery was necessary in order to find you and bring you here, in order to change things on our world for the better. My sons didn't understand when I tried to explain."

"I don't believe you. This is madness." I tremble. Confused. None of this makes sense.

"I can understand why you might not trust me just yet. But perhaps there is another whose word you might trust more?"

A man walks out from the shadows. A man I have come to know over the last few weeks. A man I thought I could trust.

"Hello, Arianna."

"Hello...Asher."

EPILOGUE

Fenris Vane

"They have unleashed the Prince of War."
—Arianna Spero

I wake with a start, my heart hammering in my chest. "Arianna!" I scream her name into the dark cave. It is cold, too cold for a human. The fire has been dead for hours, and though I can still smell Ari's scent lingering in the air, she is gone.

And she is in trouble.

Her blood pumps through me. It healed me faster than anything should have. And now, I understand why my father chose her above all others.

I need to see Asher. His answers to my questions will determine whether he keeps his head or not.

Baron whines at the entrance, and we both tear through the snow and run as fast as our legs will carry us. Her scent fades now that we are in the open. New snowfall has covered her tracks, and it doesn't take us long to lose any hope of finding her. I scream into the woods, and Baron matches my grief with his own howl.

We run back to the castle. This time I don't slow for Baron. I use all my demon strength, pushing through the pain still in me.

Once there, I immediately send scouts to search the woods, and another to bring Asher to me posthaste.

Everyone avoids me as I tear through the castle looking for any clue as to what happened to Arianna, though in my heart, I know. And it means war. More than war. It means annihilation.

When Asher arrives, he smiles at first, ready with a cocky quip. I erase that smile with my fist.

He rubs his jaw, looking confused. "That's an odd sort of greeting for your favorite brother. What troubles you, Fen?"

I step up close to him. "Tell me you didn't know."

"Didn't know what, brother?"

"That Arianna is of royal Fae blood. That you planned to marry the true heir off to one of us, thus securing our reign forever."

His eyes widen, and I know in that instant the truth. I punch him again, this time sending him flying back.

His normally jovial face turns hard. "I'll give you those, but no more, Fen. How did you find out?"

"Her blood," I say.

"You broke the oath?"

I shake my head. "Not consciously. I was poisoned by raider's blood. They mixed it with something. I nearly died. She made me feed off her while I was unconscious."

Asher frowns. "How did her blood not make you worse?"

I shrug. "I do not know. I thought you might. Perhaps it is the mix of human and Fae. Maybe it negated the poison."

"What about the other effects?" he asks.

"Those were not negated. It is still a drug. An elixir. I healed far too fast. I feel too strong."

Asher rubs his chin again. "You certainly do at that."

"Why did you not tell me who I was guarding?"

"Father said, for this to work, it had to remain secret. He said he only told me, and that I was to tell no one."

I squeeze a fist. Even in death, my father favors my brother.

Asher looks around. "Where is the princess now?"

"She's gone," I growl. "They took her while I was unconscious. I felt it. It's what woke me from the stupor."

"She is the key to everything," he says. "We must find her. Now, before we lose her forever."

My eyes fall to the ground. "Don't you see? We have already lost her. They will tell her the truth of who she is, and she will think we betrayed her. That *I* betrayed her. And we will be at war. With her as their leader."

Asher lays a hand on my arm. "You love her."

It's not a question, so I don't bother answering.

"Brother, this cannot be. You were chosen by the High Council to guard her and protect her because you refused to be king."

I look up, fury raging in me. "This isn't about being king. This is about Arianna and her life."

"She will not walk away so easily from us, brother. We still have her mother's soul. She will come back, and she will choose a prince. Or her contract will be broken and her mother's soul will spend eternity in hell."

My fist acts of its own volition, landing on Asher's jaw and knocking him out this time. I leave his body on the floor and walk away.

...

Five weeks ago, I stood in front of my father, the king, holding both our goblets of wine in my hand. Indecision plagued me.

One goblet contained poisoned wine. And how my father answered my questions would determine which goblet he received.

"You have never had a head for the long game," he said to me, in that patronizing way he always had. "You just want to stab your sword at a problem, but some things require more delicacy. More manipulation."

"You're talking about destroying your own people," I said, still holding the goblets.

My father paced the sitting room and continued to deliver his lecture about the greater good and the fate of this world and how we will never break the curse that plagues us if we don't sacrifice a few of our own.

When he asked for the wine, I gave him the goblet in my right hand.

I gave him the poison.

He drained it, and I waited for him to fall to the ground.

I expected the wrenching.

I expected the foaming at the mouth.

But I didn't expect his heart to stop.

The poison wasn't meant to kill him. It was meant to render him unconscious so he could be imprisoned and questioned further.

I acted quickly, setting the room to look as if he'd been alone, and leaving, allowing someone else to find his body.

He was declared dead.

He was interred in the mausoleum.

And I took over the hunt for his killer.

It was me the whole time.

But I didn't destroy his body. And I never under-stood how he died. Zeb's report told me one thing. My poison didn't kill him.

So what did?

Or who?

My wrist burns, pulling me out of memory and into the present. I look down at my wrist. My demon mark glows a bright red.

Arianna is summoning me. Calling me.

And I will find her.

TO BE CONTINUED

We hope you enjoyed *Vampire Girl*, the first book in this new fantasy series. Want to find out the moment the next book is available? Sign up for the Karpov Kinrade newsletter and never miss a launch. And visit KarpovKinrade.com for more great books to read.

ABOUT THE AUTHORS

Karpov Kinrade is the pen name for the husband and wife writing duo of USA TODAY bestselling, award-winning authors Lux Kinrade and Dmytry Karpov.

Together, they write fantasy and science fiction.

Look for more from Karpov Kinrade in *Vampire Girl*, *The Shattered Islands*, *The Nightfall Chronicles* and *The Forbidden Trilogy*.

They live with three little girls who think they're ninja princesses with super powers and who are also showing a propensity for telling tall tales and using the written word to weave stories of wonder and magic.

Find them at www.KarpovKinrade.com

On Twitter @KarpovKinrade

On Facebook /KarpovKinrade

And subscribe to their newsletter for special deals and up-to-date notice of new launches. www.ReadKK.com.

~~~~~

If you enjoyed this book, consider supporting the author by leaving a review wherever you purchased this book. Thank you.

CPSIA information can be obtained
at www.ICGtesting.com
Printed in the USA
LVOW01s1818031016
507217LV00026B/862/P